James
Where Did He Go?

D.W. Smith

Nora Ray Publishing

Dedication

James, a science-fiction novel is dedicated to all the multitudes of men and women with handicaps. With courage, dedication and perseverance many handicapped persons have made remarkable contributions to the well-being of mankind.

James, despite his handicap, dared to venture into the unknown, as do many, in spite of handicaps.

No one told James it couldn't be done! He just didn't!

Acknowledgments

There are no words in my limited vocabulary to express my gratitude, to my maker for long life, good health and for the privilege to write and publish.

The debt I owe, to my two deceased wives, who demanded, "Do something with that 'stuff'," goes without saying. James, now a novel, is one of that 'stuff.'

James is a science fiction novel, written solely for the entertainment of the reader. James came to life as a short story, but collected dust in a closet for many years. Recently, rewritten as a novel, "James came back!"

To my children, grandchildren and great grandchildren, to each and every one, you are a blessing from my God. Anyone of you, would be someone, anyone – would be proud of.

To Nora Ray, one of my daughters, a special thanks. Without her, and without her help, none of my books would have been published. Thank you seems so inadequate! – Again, – thank you!

To Vivian Donnigan, whose typing skills, constructive criticisms, and encouragement has been invaluable to my writing efforts.

To Nora and Vivian, with their special abilities, to read what I write in Smith hieroglyphics with creative spelling, I find truly remarkable. Thank you!

CONTENTS

PART ONE
James

CHAPTER ONE

JAMES

I tem in the local newspaper:

> According to Sherriff Davis, James McFeen, long-time resident of this county, vanished under mysterious circumstances.
>
> McFeen was reported missing by his wife early last Saturday morning. She stated that he had been "puttering" out in the barn as usual on his days off. McFeen was a second shift electrician at the local factory.
>
> Sherriff Davis stated that the investigation will continue. Special investigators have been called to assist local law enforcement.

Now that's not a name I am likely to forget. I first met James McFeen several years ago.

I had recently been promoted to third shift maintenance foreman at the local factory. When you have lots of machines and lots of people to run them, lots of things go wrong. Murphy's Law applies: Anything that can go wrong, will go wrong, at the most inopportune moment!

The first rule of the jungle for a maintenance foreman is get it fixed – FAST – technicalities, according to management and production are excuses. Folks standing around is lost production – Fix It! How it gets fixed isn't important. To production, down time knocks their world off its axis. Maintenance's job is to keep their world spinning.

Rule number two, for all mechanic men at a large factory, is overworked, underpaid, and the hours are way too long.

Rule number three, you never have enough bodies to get the job done!

The maintenance superintendent came by for a little chit chat. "I hired you a new man for a replacement on your team. He's kind of young, you know, you take what you can get these days. His name is James McFeen. It should be McNuts or something. Anyway, catch him at the time clock tomorrow night if he shows up."

The next night I'm standing down by the time clock counting bodies, wondering how many of my crew will show up. At last there is the lost goose. They always look like a goose flying north while all the flock is flying south for the winter.

"You James McFeen?" I asked.

"Uh, yes'ser dey' sez tu come in dat door and somebody ud meets me. Is you da boss?"

Lord Help! He just came into town and fell off the turnip truck! Where do they get those folks, I pondered. "I'm the maintenance foreman. Some of the men call me boss, others, call me a lot of other things."

I told him my name and proceeded to show him around. "The man you are to replace was an old hand. He knew this place upside down. He moved on and I'm shorthanded. You know anything about electricity?" I asked.

"Some," says he.

"Know the difference between AC and DC?" I asked.

"Uh yes'ser, little bit," says he.

"Ever worked in the field?" I asked.

"Some," he says.

"Where'd you work?" I asked.

"Kurt's Electric," says he.

Lord God, I'm pulling teeth. "What'd you do for Kurt?" I asked.

"Mostly pulled wire and stuff in houses," says he.

"Why'd you leave Kurt?" I asked.

Don't like Kurt," says he.

While we're having this enlightening conversation I noticed he was taking everything around him in. "You ever worked in a factory before?" I asked.

"Nope," says he, "Shore hopes I can makes it 'roun here."

"How old are you?" I asked.

"Twenty two," says he.

"Where'd you go to school?" I asked.

"Bowling," says he.

"Bowling? Why that's a Middle School. Did you go to High School?" stunned I asked.

"Nope," says he.

"Why?" I asked.

"Don't like school, never did," says he.

"How did you learn about electricity?" I asked. All the time thinking where in the world did they dig up this bozo?

"Read some books," says he.

"That all." I demanded.

"Oh, I likes messin' around 'lectricity some," says he.

In short order my education really began. James took to factory maintenance like a duck took to water. He seemed to have a knack of finding solutions to problems. Some, I swore, came from the twilight zone. His intent curiosity was boundless. Machines and how they worked, or, why they didn't work, never seemed to faze him. All the time James always looked like he wasn't paying attention. As a maintenance foreman, I soon discovered he was a God's send. Amen.

Over the next several years, I developed a deep fond relationship with James. He was just different, an odd duck to say the least.

One day in a leisure moment I asked James, "What goes through that head of yours all the time?

"Not much, I guess," says he.

"You seem to be preoccupied of late, is something wrong?" I asked.

"Well," says he. "I's been a thinkin' 'bout flying saucers of late, you know those things in the news lately."

I just asked a question I wished I hadn't asked, however knowing James; I just couldn't let that be. "What about flying saucers?" I asked. With James, I just don't know what to expect.

"Well," says he, "I's been thinkin' on `um of lates, thinks I's gots `um figgered out."

Now if anyone else on the face of the earth had said that to me, it would have gone in one ear and out the other to outer space. But, James said it. Somehow James saying such things was different. His words went in both my ears and crashed somewhere in the middle.

"Well, I'd like to hear your thinking on flying saucers." I was certain, friend or not, he had flipped out! But then I had known James for a year or so and seen him in operation more than once. I've gotta take this with a grain of salt!

I was reminded of a story I heard years ago about a gambler. He cautioned "If a man tells you he can make the Jack of clubs jump out of a deck of cards and spit cider in your eye, be careful, you may get cider in your eye. Some men just have a way of doing things different."

"OK, James you got my attention, lay it on me." I said, then added, "If there is such a thing as UFO and Aliens, where did they come from?"

"Don't know, don't care" said he, "It's the saucer I'm interested in." he reflected a minute. "I think 'them' machines that run's on gravity, that's all there is to it. I think I know how they work."

Whoo, James had just reduced Physics and Math to a nut shell. "It's simple," says he, "Flying Saucers are anti-gravitrons."

"Anti-gravitrons", I ask in utter amazement, don't know that word, "what's anti-gravitrons?"

"It's a motor that runs on gravity. You know about 'lectric motors, there's round machines that run on 'lectric, saucers run on anti-gravity. That's it!"

He explained, "That's why saucers are round, they are anti-gravity motors."

The simplicity of James's explanation made my head spin.

If it's so simple why didn't I think of it? I now know, and understand, in vivid detail, how I wasted a college education. James just explained the mysteries of UFO's in terms I can understand – well maybe – now I'm taking lessons!

"You know about magnets," said James. "They have a north and a south pole. Put two norths or two souths together they repel one another. But put south and north together, they attract each other. Same with gravity, gravity attracts anything 'different' positive gravity is one pole everything else is negative. That's why they attract. All you got to do is make an anti-gravity machine." James paused briefly, and then adds, "I'm working on one at my place."

Of all the men I've ever known or worked with, James defied all orthodox explanations. At some times he was the simplest of the simple – or profoundly complex. He just defied reason. On the one hand he was an open book, on the other, a Gordian knot.

Men fear most what they understand least. Fear, more often than not, became anger and ridicule when applied to James. James had a knack for scaring people. Yet, he was without a doubt, one of the gentlest, unassuming, people I have ever known.

In short order, he became an integral part of my maintenance team, yet, always set apart. For me, he was dependable, able and helpful. But there always seemed to be something missing. He just wasn't quite with the program.

With his co-workers, they just tolerated him. Yet, they depended on him when things went wrong! He was just better at solving problems. Somehow he just never seemed to have a problem that was unsolvable. Nor did he ever need help. He seemed to be more machine than man. He didn't talk much. His answers were always short and to the point. He rarely smiled and always seemed aloft. Only James, was James.

In the year or so that I worked with James, he became my

able assistant. When I needed special help, he always seemed nearby, and was willing. No matter how difficult or exasperating the task, he never complained, and never quit. In short, sometimes I wondered if he was human. He never needed coffee breaks, smoke breaks, and never went to the bathroom – he just worked at the task. James had an uncanny ability to learn new ways of doing things. Skills, some of us took years to develop, James became proficient in a day. As foreman I must admit, James became invaluable to me, but his seeming loyalty to me became somewhat unnerving. Whether it was my stature as boss, my tolerance of his peculiarities, or my needs, certainly not my good looks, whatever it was, I was thankful for James.

CHAPTER TWO
NEW JOB

After a couple of years, I was reassigned as maintenance foreman of second shift. The hours suited me much better, but with the new job became more responsibilities, and a new crew. I had just gotten the rough edges off the third shift crew, except for James, and now I had to start all over, as the new kid on the block. Factory workers are never too keen on any new ways, or new bosses. Especially if the new bosses job is to speed up the system. Be that as it may, let the wars begin!

After a while my shift and crew began to settle down. One or two decided I was an idiot, two or three more a tyrant, and to the rest just a cross to bear, in my world, just business as usual.

Part of my new responsibilities, was the task of relaying the new directives from 'higher ups' to maintenance on third shift. Somehow lots of things get lost in translation, from first shift, to second shift, to graveyard. The third shift is known as graveyard because; in the middle of the night everybody is dead or at least unresponsive. Anyway, by sunrise, first shift will arrive and third shift can go to sleep.

Sometime later, I got my instruction from the 'Soup' to pass onto third shift. I found Jerry, the new third shift foreman, in the midst of a machine calamity. Something had unraveled.

Been there. Done that. All's well that ends well, that is, as long as you can ignore production. The peace and quiet usually erupts in about two seconds. The machine operator wants it fixed – Now – No yesterday!

"Jerry" I said, "Need a little help?"

"Oh Yeah, I haven't been here long enough to learn this piece of worn out junks peculiarities." "It's electrical, and James McNut's is down on eight looking lost. Can you do something quick?" Jerry begged.

I opened the control panel, and espied the broken rubber band, "This thing runs on a rubber band?" I said.

I smiled at Jerry, in his bewilderment. "This is a James quick fix secret." With an air of 'all knowing,' I added, "Don't ask why, just thank the God's of rubber bands."

I selected the proper breaker in the panel, pulled the switch down, then back up, and stretched the new rubber band, from the switch to a screw head up above. The lights blinked, the line sprung into life, and the products began to move.

Another barb at Jerry was in order, "See how simple that was. Someday before you retire, or die of old age, production will schedule some down time, and then you can replace the breaker. In the meantime, don't run out of rubber bands!"

I smirked, "By the way, this is a, what you know thing, not what you do. That's why we get the big bucks."

"Rubber Bands" Jerry mumbled.

I related to Jerry the latest decrees from the powers that be, as our conversation ended, Jerry went about his tasks, and I headed for the time clock. As I turned about to leave, I saw James coming my way, exhibiting one of his rare smiles.

"How goes things for you?" I asked.

"Not good," says he.

Did I dare ask, "What's wrong?"

"Not the same. Youse gone," says he.

"But I thought you liked it here." I observed.

"Did, don't now. New boss don't like me," says he, "thinks I'm stupid."

"Stupid" I repeated James's word. "James," I said, "I have thought a lot of things about you since I've known you, but stupid is not one of them. I will say you are not like any man I've ever known and you take some getting used to, but stupid you certainly are not!"

"You let me work, new boss don't." a pause, James adds "Not like you."

Here I knew I'd better change the subject. "By the way" I asked, "How's the saucer thing working out for you?"

A blank look, a pause, and then again that rare James smile, "I been working on it" say he.

Four or five months passed in the never, never land of maintenance. Nothing is ever right, everything is wrong according to management and production. The 'Soup' passed the good word to me, "The changes you made on third shift, has caused a problem. It seems production on third shift has had a substantial increase. Now they are making more production than paint can paint. Got any ideas?"

"Maybe, I'll think on it." I said.

"Oh, yeah, I got a request from James McFeen for a transfer to second shift. Jerry says he can do without him, you want him? I hear you two get along fine," said Soup.

"You can send him my way," I smiled.

CHAPTER THREE

FIX IT

J ames's arrival on second shift was about like it was on third shift. He was useful, but just didn't quite fit in. If or when he talked, it was about motors. "Anti-Gravitrons" those conversations left most folks with a blank look on their face, then a shake of their head, and a reply "Uh-Hu"

Still James had a knack for getting a machine back in operation. If electrical, most are, he could zero in on the problem and devise a solution, sometimes, unorthodox, all the time, in his own private world. Looking like he was somewhere else. In maintenance, results count, looks don't.

The maintenance supervisor, "Soup" came into my world, looking like he had lost his last friend. "Jack" the plant manager, wants us in his office tomorrow before your shift starts, say about 12:00 o'clock.

Usually when Jack had something to say to me he'd be around the time clock when I came in. Usually it would be something he wanted me to look into. Some machine, somewhere, production said needed attention.

Usually that was the last I would hear from Jack, until the next complaint surfaced. Otherwise the only thing he had to say to me was the latest stupid joke he had heard. Where Jack came up with all those bad jokes was beyond me. Bad jokes, I guess, was his way of a compliment, or was it shock treatment?

The next day I came to the 'Soups' office a little early to get the low down. 'Soup' was pacing the floor like a caged animal.

"Whasup?" I asked.

"I just hate these things; there are all kind of muckity mucks around here today. They came from the corporate office in Chicago, for a powwow. Me, you, and Roger Rabbit, were invited. God knows who else. Let's go." 'Soup' smiled, and took off with me trying to keep up.

We took the short stroll to Jack's office, the door was open, and we cautiously went in.

Jack was talking to the men I had heard about, but had never expected to see in this lifetime, the corporate CEO, the general secretary, Roger and somebody. That somebody in time would become a thorn in everybody's side.

The CEO was a very elderly man, he had started the company years ago, maintenance control had made it into the Corporation it now was. A Corporation many of us working stiffs liked, as far as I knew, he didn't interfere with progress.

Jack introduced 'Soup' and I to the Big Boss. This is our maintenance superintendent, 'Soup'.

"Yes, I've met 'Soup' before, good job." said Big Bossman.

This is our second shift maintenance foreman, known around here as 'Head of the Misfits.' 'Misfits' I thought was an inside local joke devised by Jack, in reference to me and my crew.

"We've heard of the 'Misfits' good job. Now down to business" said Mr. No Nonsense Big Boss.

"It has come to our attention," said Mr. Big Boss, "that

dramatic improvement in production, in this plant has been made. Our thanks and congratulations are in order. Thank you and Congratulations! We at home office will expect a detailed report on how the improvements were made, in the next few days. That about covers it."

'Soup' and I left the meeting. It was over before it ever started.

I demanded of 'Soup" as we walked back to his office "What's that Misfit stuff? Is that me or my crew?"

"Both," 'Soup' smiled, "Everybody knows that you and two or three of that crew are Misfits, to say the least. However that improvement you all made in streamlining paint and on line efficiency was noteworthy.

"Jack told 'em up north. By the way, thanks. Now we are all in trouble! How'd you get it done, with that bunch?" "Soup" asked.

"It was easy" I said, "I just told them what the problem was and said "Fix it". Tell me before you blow the place up. So I can strike the match. None of that bunch knew it couldn't be done, I didn't tell 'em."

I met my crew as they came in; I sent them down to the electric shop. "Wait till I get there" I ordered. The last man came in and we walked the few steps to the 'lectric shop. There they were, all the Misfits in one wad, in one moment in time.

Somebody piped up, "Did you get to see the Big Boss from Chicago?" "Was he as mean as they say?" "Did he have horns?" "What'd they say?"

"Alright you Misfits," I demanded. "Now you're famous, they know about you in Chicago. Big Boss said good job, and thanks, next time do better. Write a report, anyone of you misfits knows how to write?" I asked.

No reply, just silence, at last.

"If we's famous, we's gonna gets more money?" James – James of all people made a joke. We all stood there stunned. A moment of reverence then laughter!

"They didn't talk about money," I said "They talked about written reports, anyone of you Misfits know how to write? Speak up" I ordered. At that they scattered like Quail.

Now that I think about it, I can't write reports either. "I hope 'Soup' can write" I said to myself.

CHAPTER FOUR

GRAVITON

From time to time when all was quiet in production's world, we of what became known as the Misfits would have our moments to enjoy each other, as men at war, even if it was just a maintenance war.

Now and then James would ask me rather pointed questions. "Boss how'd you learn about motors and microwaves, machines and stuff like that? Is that stuff you's learned in college?"

"Not really," I said, "It started back when I was in the sixth grade, and I had a teacher that got me started. In Science class, we ordered a little electric motor kit for kids. For a quarter you could get this little kit that made an electric motor that ran on a 'C' Battery."

All it was, was some crooked pieces of iron, some copper wire, and some instructions. I built my first motor. I was thrilled to death. When I hooked it up to the battery that Whuuuuur was about all the excitement I could stand.

After class I took my twenty five cent motor home. I wondered what it would do with two batteries. AH-HA what about three? Wow, look at it go! Four batteries produced my first lesson "Oops! Wish I hadn't done that!" The little motor went up in smoke.

Next thing was build a bigger version, I had a pattern, I made a new bigger version, and took it to school for show and tell.

As long as I can remember, I made things. But an electric motor was something, my teacher said. A bright boy like you should read a book about making things. Like radios and things. Wow, that's for me!

The next thing, at Christmas, our neighbor put out a Santa Claus that would talk to kids. I wanted to know how he could talk. "You a dummy" I said, "How can you talk?"

"You're that kid next door, aren't you?" said Santa. "Come up to the house and I'll show you how Santa can talk."

Mr. Thompson was a genius, I was sure of that. He said "See this speaker, when I flip this switch this ways it's a microphone, that way it's a speaker, there's one just like it by Santa. When the switch is this way, the one here is a speaker, that one out by Santa is a mike. Flip the switch, this one becomes a mike and that one becomes a speaker. Mikes and speakers are basically the same thing. You just got to know which way they are working. That bunch of tubes, capacitors and resistors makes it work." A mystery unraveled in kid talk, I was amazed.

I just kept building contraptions as best I could. Next, came a science project, for the local science fair. I was second, but got to go to State. I came in fourth, and my classmate won State, with a homemade photo cell, and went to Nationals. They made a fuss about two kids from the same science class going so far. The science teacher was some sort of hero.

"Then I discovered rockets, girls and cars all about the same time." I added, "I still like rockets, girls and cars, but the order has changed now and then.

"I was just barely eighteen when I graduated from high school, in two years. Dad and Mom had their heart set on me going to college, 'I'm tired of school.' I announced. The next day after graduation, I decided to go into the service, and learn a trade.

"I lit on the Army, three years enlistment instead of four. After Basic Training, I went to school to learn how to repair electronic devices. I never saw so much so quickly in my life. How I made it through school I'll never know. Then off to the exotic Far East, to get shot at. That's when it dawned on me that you could get killed over here.

"When I got back to the states, I got my thirty day leave, a new assignment, a new school, and a new wife. What else did I need at twenty years old?

"My new assignment was a ground to air Missile Battalion. After a short school, I was to teach elementary classes in guided missiles, how the radar worked and how to fix it. I lost interest real quick!

"I found a buddy with a Drag Race Car. He let me drive it once. That was nearly as much fun as my new young wife. Cars became a passion, work a necessity. Race cars and wives were expensive.

"What about you?" I asked. "How's the saucer working out? I've not heard you talk about it lately."

Then came that distant look, "Uh, I'm working on it," James said.

In a quiet time James asked, "you 'fraid of dying, or gettin' hurt in that race car?"

"Not really," I said, "When I buckle up and my motor is running I'm too busy to be scared."

"Why you do it?" James asked.

"You really want to know?" I asked, "The truth or the lie?"

I saw confusion in James's face. "Uh, uh, truth I guess. You's means there's both?"

"The truth is I'm not sure why. The lie is I know exactly why I do it. I have to know which is which, only I don't always know until the race is over. My best was truth." I said.

"The best competitor I ever competed against pointed out that if you're really good, you don't have to cheat to win, it's the race that's important. Most folks sit on the sidelines and cheer or boo. I don't, I do my best. In time, with practice and effort, I got good at car racing.

"People who can't do or won't do, what you can do, are by far your nastiest critics. At times unreasonable, but those of us that have developed a skill, are not your critics, we're fellow soldiers, Misfits.

"James, I've been a Misfit all my life. It wasn't until a teacher and a little electric motor kit, showed me the truth. I didn't have to cheat to win, just get good. You won't win all your races, but you will never lose.

"James," I asked, "are you still working on your saucer?"

"Still working on it," says he.

"How long you been at it?" I asked.

"`Bout three years or so," says he.

"Are you making progress?" I asked.

Maybe," says he.

James was never a wealth of information; rarely would

he volunteer much about what he knew. I was astounded at those rare times when he decided to say something.

"Don't believe the Big Bang Theory is right." James volunteered.

"Uh-Hu" I said, I wasn't prepared for a discussion I didn't know much about. I was just about to show my ignorance. "What's wrong with the Big Bang Theory?" Did I dare ask that question?

"Well," says he, "First off an anti-gravitron wouldn't work, but they do. According to the Big Bang, Gravity pulled all the mass of the universe into the size of a hickory nut, then it exploded. After the Big Bang, how much gravity was determined by how much mass came together. Ain't that right?"

"Uh-Hu," I said, I didn't have a clue if "Ain't that right" was a question or an answer. I clutched for a celestial straw, "You said, an anti-gravitron wouldn't work, but say anti-gravity does? How do you know?" I asked dumb founded.

"I made one," says he.

"Uh-Hu, when? `Um, how'd you do that?" I unwittingly asked.

"I got a little one made, when I turned it on, it went through the roof of my workshop. Won't come back. No controls in it."

"Uh-Hu" Now I have been accused of a lot of things in my life, having good sense hasn't been one of them very often. I had known James for about six years when this conversation took place. It's my considered opinion, me and James are both nuts, him for saying such things, and me for considering the possibility of James's claim.

In the six years that I had known him, I never once saw or heard of him saying or doing anything unacceptable, but this anti-gravitron, and saucer thing, scared me. Maybe I do fear what I know least.

CHAPTER FIVE
THE WHEELS FALL OFF

My factory world was about to come apart, for the seven years I had been here, I worked at a job I liked. I liked the people that worked for me and I really liked the people I answered to. In this plant, the plant manager, Jack, and the maintenance superintendent "Soup" gave me a job to do, then left me alone to do it. When problems arose between maintenance and production, Jack and 'Soup' were referee and judge. In factory work, that conflict escalates to all-out war at times. The new production Chief, Roger the Jack Ass, was sure that all he had to do was order more production, maintenance knows better. Machines wear out, break, or just lay down and die. Those are technicalities and excuses, according to Roger Rabbit, and scheduled down time is lost production. Let the wars begin!

The new production Chief was a fellow that when things went wrong, it was someone else's fault. "Yes sir, your right" was all he wanted to hear, anything else was foot dragging or incompetence.

"To add fuel to the fire, he observes James working on a machine looking lost. He had to be the most incompetent Jack Ass in the plant! He had to go!" Said Roger Jackass.

That did it, the war was on. I served notice that maintenance and the second shift Misfits were my problem, not his. He would probably be better scheduling production on working machines.

Things had been going pretty well for me for the past seven years, but all was about to change in short order. 'Soup' came by for a little chat, and said, "Guess you heard Big Boss is about dead, and has turned the business over to Sonny. Sonny is not like Big Boss. He's sixty-seven years old, never done a day's work in his life. The story goes, Big Boss, gave Sonny a million dollars for every grandkid, Sonny's been busy making kids, ten or twelve I hear. Anyway, he and the general secretary are in charge now. Big changes are in the works."

I had met Big Boss and the general secretary, at the command performance I had attended in Jack's office, with 'Soup', several years ago. I discovered I had met Sonny too. He was that somebody from Chicago, the soon to be thorn in everybody's side.

The wheels of the God's began to turn, "Jack wants us up in his office. Now," ordered 'Soup'. In the seven years I had worked for 'Soup' I had never heard an order like that.

We went to Jacks office in a hurry, more like a trot than a walk. When we arrived, Jack was obviously agitated.

"Sit down" Jack demanded. "I got orders from Chicago. They have decided to increase production at this plant. We have been selected because of the streamlining that took place. A new addition is to be made holding six new lines." A pause, while color came back to Jack's face "Here is the part that will thrill you two to death."

Jack pointed his finger at 'Soup' "You are ordered liaison between here and Chicago. All matters here will be reported to the general secretary, and you," he pointed at me, "Will be in charge of construction." "And me, I'm sure will shortly be replaced. Don't ask me any questions, all answers come from Chicago." Jack added, "That's that, Good – Bye!"

That was not that, and it was not good-bye, but Hello New World!" "Jack" I said, "who took that vote."

"Chicago did." Jack replied. "I was not asked, I was told, and my job now is to relay decrees."

This didn't set well with me. "If I'm to build a new production line, who do I answer to, you, 'Soup' or Chicago?"

Jack said, "I'll take it up with Chicago."

Just about every factory worker I know or have ever known, works in the factory for the paycheck. It supports their real reason for living, that's NOT the Factory! We just work for the paycheck. The fringe benefit is if you like your job.

Jack's real life was golf, and hunting up new stupid jokes to tell. 'Soups' were his farm, black cows, and aggravating me about running fifteen laps on three wheels.

I guess I need to explain that. I lost the inside front wheel, under full acceleration, it doesn't touch the ground much anyway, the front left wheel just holds up a corner of the car, when the car's not moving. According to 'Soup' that's how to fix machines, leave the lug nut off and run on three wheels.

Loyal fans are always a delight. Anyway, cars were a passion when I went to work at the factory. The factory kept me, my family and my race car in the style we were accustomed to living in.

With the Misfits, there was a cowboy, a fitness freak, a partyer, a loud mouth, and James to name a few.

James volunteered one day, "Me's and Margaret went to the car races last Saturday. The 'nouncer said, "You's quittin racin'. Yous'll be missed.   You's got smart in old age?" my word, a

James smile and funny in the same day.

"Margaret," I asked, "whose Margaret?"

"Woman I's found likes me, we's gettin' married. You's want to come?"

"Wouldn't miss it on a bet." I smiled, "This'll get your mind off saucers for a while. When's this happening?"

He gave me the when, and where, and what time then added, "You's house building all time now? Me too, getting wife, like you."

My, My, what did that mean in James language? I'd better let that be. I guess time will tell.

I got home at a decent hour, my wife was still up. "Honey," I said, "We been invited to a wedding, James McFeen is getting married next Saturday."

"You mean that screwball that came out here and fixed the TV antenna at one o'clock in the morning, while you held the flashlight? Who'd marry him?" she snarled.

"Somebody like you." I kidded her. "You married me."
At the wedding I discovered I must live in a vacuum, because I didn't hear or know anything. The Bride was a production worker, on one of the lines, eight I think. I had seen her, a pleasant, plain girl. There were a couple hundred young, pleasant, plain girls working here. The Best Man I knew, a second shift Misfit, and the Daddy that gave her away was, Robert Green, one of my 'old' Misfits. I knew he had kids, I didn't know Margaret was one of them.

The Bride looked the best she could, and James looked scared to death, and the preacher had a good time at the expense of the Bride and Groom. Even 'Soup' was there. I didn't know that 'Soup' and James were that close.

"I didn't know that James invited you" I said to 'Soup'.

"He didn't," said 'Soup' "Margaret's daddy did. We came up through the ranks together. How else could I know what you Misfits were up to? He's the only one of your bunch that is anything like normal."

'Soup' was enjoying himself at my expense. That was the 'Soup' I knew he was usually around at his men's weddings and funerals.

CHAPTER SIX
BEGINNER'S LUCK

'S oup' became a factor in my life, from the first day I set foot in the factory. I needed a job, any job, now. And I couldn't leave town to get one, I had to stay here at least for a while. My mother was terminally ill, in the final stages; the place I had been working went Bankrupt and closed. And the race track closed for the season. I needed a job, Now.

One of my racing buddies said he heard they needed line mechanics, out at the factory. "Maybe they'll hire you, they're always shorthanded, I hear."

I went in the door that said applicants, a young lady handed me a job application, and said, "What job are you applying for?"

"A maintenance job, I guess." I said.

"We have an opening I think on third shift, would you be interested?" she asked.

"Yes" I said.

"Fill out the application, I'll be right back, in a few minutes" she said as she vanished through the door, that said employees only.

After a few minutes she returned and said "The Maintenance Superintendent, will see you if you can wait."

"I can wait" I said, "Thank you."

After a while a man came through the door, that said, employees. I stood up as he neared me, he extended his hand. "They call me 'Soup'," he said, "You looking for a maintenance job. Is that your application?" he asked.

"Yes sir" I said. I handed him the paper.

"Let's go down to my office for a bit" he said.

"He's a farmer" I thought, "Those Brogan shoes, and chewing tobacco gave him away, Lord Help."

"Set down while I look over your application," he said.

I set down in the folding chair, on one side of the table full of junk. He sat down in the other chair, on the other side. I took a quick glance around, junk everywhere, wall to wall junk.

"Uh-Hu, Vet, Army, three years. Computer operator programmer, two years, Air craft, five years, Mill Wright, four years. Education: BA, Post Grad. Wife, three boys. "Got you beat, I got four" he said, "anything else?"

"Well," I said, "I taught school for a year." "And tied steel out at the Bridge plant, while I was in college."

"Uh-Hu," he stared at me for a moment, "What's your degree?" he asked.

"Pre Law, Post Grad education" I said softly.

"Uh-Hu, You been busy ain't you!" a pause, "Law won't help you here" a questioning stare, "You wouldn't be that guy that got shot over in the next town, or the wild one that drives a car out at the race track?"

"Well," I said, "I haven't been shot at in several years. But, I've been known to drive Jalopy now and then."

"I saw that three wheel race you run. I thought you had a chance to win, until you got in traffic. Anyway the crowd and PA man liked it." "By the way" 'Soup' asked, "With your credentials, why are you applying for a job here? Top pay here is about half of Air Craft. I worked on U-Twos, before I came here. Work a while, get a good job, get laid off." A pause, "Then start over."

"That's about how it's worked for me, along with my folks dying! My mother is terminally ill, there's no one to see to her, except me and Grandma. There's no one else! In the short term, I'll take what I can get." Surely that was not begging, I thought.

"Uh-Hu, well, I understand that," he said, "I don't figure you'll last long, but I'll give you a try. When can you start?"

"Now" I said.

"Your shift starts at ten o'clock; I'll meet you at the time clock. Come through the south door." 'Soup' added, "any questions?"

"Not now," I said, "Thanks, I'll be here."

'Soup' met me at the door, showed me my time card location, and explained procedures. "I'll show you around." 'Soup' stated, "We got four maintenance men on this shift, we need ten, your number five. There's twelve production lines, each line takes eight to twelve people. Crazies all on fork lifts – I don't want you on one, I've seen you drive." – was that another dig?

We toured the electric shop, the machine shop, the welding shop, and then he asked, "You know how to run any of these machines?" "Like lathes, Heli Arcs, Bridge Port…"

"Most of em." I said.

"Well, don't tear nutthin' up." 'Soup' said.

I met the Production Supervisor, and Head of Quality Control, and the other four macanics'. "Their pretty good men, but none of them are comfortable with electricity. We've started upgrading the power on lines, from DC drives to AC frequency modulation. Anyway the head electrician and I are about all we got to work on the New Stuff. I'm going to turn you over to the dogs, stay close to the mechanics for a while, 'til you get your feet on the ground. Don't let the wolves eat you alive on your first night. I just about live out here now, when production just has to have some machine – can't live without it, me or somebody comes out in the middle of the night. Otherwise it's down till the next day and production is screaming like banshees. Anyway, you'll soon know if you last. See you tomorrow, Lord willing!"

I followed somebody around the first couple of nights, getting oriented, getting familiar with the jargon; usually old stuff is called by names you've never heard before, Most of the production lines hardware I was familiar with.

As a Mill Wright, I had built a lot of similar stuff. It was all in a day's work. Their hardware was mostly run of the mill for me; the new drives were a little tricky. It had been years since I had been called upon to repair a Hysteresis Drive, but radar sets used a similar devise.

About my third day, one of the new drives were down, Production went into a tailspin. The head Mechanic and I were talking 'Shop' when the Production Supervisor appeared, "It stopped, can you fix it, or do I need to call "Soup"?" he demanded.

"Want me to have a look at it?" I asked. Then added, "Maybe I can help."

"We don't mess with that Beast, that's 'Soup' and Herb's toy." Robert said. "Anyway, I'll show you. All I know about that Beast is where it's at."

The control panel cabinet was locked for security. "Where's the key?" I asked.

"Probably down in 'Soups' office." "You know what you're doing?" Robert asked, concerned.

"Maybe" I said.

"If you don't, we'll all get fired." Robert pointed out.

"Is there a multi meter around here?" I asked.

I followed Robert to 'Soups' office to get the keys then to the electric shop and found a multi meter.

I opened the cabinet, and spied the schematic in the door enclosure. "That looks like a TV set, what now?" Robert asked.

I unfolded the schematic diagram, located the test points, and took a reading. Located the proper solenoid, and unplugged it, "Where can I find this animal?" I asked Robert.

'Soups' office or the electric shop." Robert said.

After a few minutes we located the right solenoid, I plugged it in and turned the power back on, after locking the panel. "See if she'll go." I said to the machine tender.

He pushed the button, the line began to hum. "Well, I'll be damned. How'd you do it?" Robert asked.

"Beginner's luck." I said.

The next night 'Soup' met me at the time clock. How'd it go around here last night? 'Soup' asked, with a kind of sheepish grin.

"Uh, I guess, OK." I said, "Kinda see what's going on around here now."

"By the way, who told you to fix that Beast?" 'Soup" asked.

"Uh, nobody, it went down, I thought maybe I'd see what was wrong with it. Nobody told me not to fix it." I said, not knowing or apologizing.

'Soup' grinned, "Now, we got a new set of problems, the log said the Beast was down sixteen minutes, it usually takes an hour or two at best, to get it back on line. The line folks got sixteen minutes of Butt time, in the Break room, instead of two hours. Keep that up and they'll put a bounty on your ears and tail. Not only that, but I got to sleep all night. What next?"

"Lucky I guess" I said.

"Well, I sure would like to rub your lucky rabbit's foot sometime" 'Soup' said.

I had worked at the factory about a month when, 'Soup made one of his appearances. There was that sheepish grin again, 'Soup' smiled "Is there any end of the trouble you're causing me? If I wasn't sleeping nights, I couldn't take it. According to the old bird that does the Heli Arcing around here. Somebody has been messing around with his Heli Arc machine. All this time I thought it belonged to the company. Anyway, the frequency setting was wrong for aluminum. Somebody told him, the new boy on third shift, had used it. He went back and looked at that sprocket you fused together. Now he's mad at the world, and I didn't even know it made a difference."

"It was magnesium, not aluminum." I interrupted.

"Not only that, but that line was only down an hour, when it should have been down for a day or two, on top of that, production on third shift is rivaling that of second shift. Now second shift is mad, even Jack is catching flack now. By the way, you look tired, how's mama?" 'Soup' asked.

"Not good," I said, "The doctor says she'll be gone soon."

"I feel for you. Get some rest." 'Soup' said.

CHAPTER SEVEN
DONKEY BAR-B-Q

A few days later, my world unraveled. I stayed at the hospital till about six, mama was barely responsive, "Go home, get some rest." she whispered, "Go home, I love you."

I slept a couple of hours and went to work. An hour or so later, the Production Secretary, came to me, "Your wife is on the phone." she whispered, with, visible tears. My heart stopped beating, I knew why mama said, "Go home."

"Trembling, I called 'Soup'; she's gone I need to leave." I whimpered.

"Go home, we'll talk later. Can I help?" 'Soup' my new friend asked.

At my mother's funeral, everything became surreal for me, but still I was aware of the presence of 'Soup' and his wife, Jack and his wife, and Robert and his wife. In my confusion and selfishness, I wondered who was running the store, with all the people sixty miles from the factory. Didn't they have anything better to do, than attend a funeral for someone they didn't know? In time, I knew, they cared.

"I'm glad to see you back," 'Soup' said. "Are you really ready to go back to work? The funeral was yesterday."

"I really need to work," I said, "nothing else means much to me right now. When I'm working, everything else vanishes, just my work matters. It's kind of like getting shot at in a war, or driving a race car, just this moment matters. I guess it's being small minded. Staying alive is a lot harder than dying."

"We'll talk later," said 'Soup', "but it'll wait."

The next night Jack was at the time clock, greeting the workers as they came in like a politician, campaigning for office. I wondered about his campaigning, he'd pop up at all hours, in all places. But usually there was such a commotion around him that everybody knew he was around. He seemed to want everybody to know he was around. What was most startling to me was he knew everybody by name, their spouse's name, and their kid's names. It was just perplexing to me, especially since I can't remember my own name half the time. How's he do that I wondered, and why?

Jack smiled at me, as I came in, "Say have you heard about the guy that drove that three wheel car?" Jack paused, "He finished the race, and came back to work. Glad your back." He patted my shoulder. "Take care." He said, and then he started up a conversation with someone else.

I just went to work: half amused, half annoyed, at the same time. I wondered, does the whole world know about three wheel cars; are all the bats out tonight? Hmm, I wonder.

Robert and Jerry was having a conversation about line five, when I walked up. They both grinned like canaries that swallowed the cat. "We got it figured out," Robert said, "those four, five days that you were gone, things didn't go to smooth. The Beast took a nap, some of the others just quit, now your back, and things are quieter. With lots of down time, the production people set down in the Break Room and figured it out, It's simple, machines are afraid of you. That's all there is to it!"

The bats are definitely out tonight. Must be the full moon, now, I've threatened race cars with trips to the scrap heap on numerous occasions, I never thought they paid any attention to me. Maybe I need to rethink the unthinkable.

I had been back to work a couple of weeks, things were getting back to normal for me. 'Soup' was out for a look see as was his habit from time to time. He usually made a point of talking to all his men on those occasions. When it came my turn, he said to me, "Jack is up in his office and wants to talk to us. They can do without you for a while." We headed to Jack's office.

"What's up," I asked.

"Donkey Bar-B-Q, you're the donkey." 'Soup' was having fun again at my expense.

Jack's door was open, we walked in. "Sit down" he said, "Be with you donkey's in a minute." He went back to looking at whatever it was he was looking at when we came in.

"It says here your ninety day probation period is about up. The company has to decide to send you packing - or give you a raise. 'Soup' and I have talked about you quite a bit of late. We don't know exactly what to do with you. You're a Misfit, so here's what we decided to do; now this is going to cause us some trouble. "We've decided," a pause that went on forever, "to offer you a new job, third shift Maintenance Foreman, here's the problem, you're not even an employee, until you have been here ninety days. On top of that, you'll be over several senior employees', who are sure you are cheating somehow, to get a job they have earned. 'Soup' and I hear the screams of foul ball already, and you will be like a cotton share cropper, when the boll weevil's eat the crop. Now the rent's due, and you got no money.

If you take us up on this idiotic offer, 'Soup' is who you answer to. I got to explain this to Chicago.

"Oh yeow, money, I'll do what I can. Chicago thinks promotions are their business, ninety day wonders will get their attention." Said Jack.

"Can I think about this, maybe talk to my wife?" I stammered.

"You got till Thursday, that's your ninety-first day, or, day one as a real employee in never, never land, if you last that long." Jack said.

"Thanks for the offer," I said, "Thanks again." 'Soup' and I left Jack's office.

Smiling, 'Soup' said, "I'm tired of this place, especially these hours. I like sleeping all night. I seem to get to sleep more now, so does Herb. We voted for you, Jack voted for you. The production totals were up. You make him look good; besides, Rose thinks you're cute, because the machines are scared of you. You slay Dragons and tame wild Beasts. With those votes, how could you go wrong?"

"I haven't voted yet, my vote is the one that counts." I said.

CHAPTER EIGHT
GREEN SMOKE

I voted to stay seven years ago, sometimes I wonder why. This is certainly one of those times.

It seemed to me that somewhere there was an election, and I was voted into an office I hadn't run for. I admit the idea of building a new production line, had some appeal for me, but I didn't get to vote evidentially, 'Soup' or Jack didn't get a vote either.

This was another time when only my vote was going to count, and I had every intention of voting, even if it hair lipped Sonny, and the General Secretary. I like a good job, I don't like politics, and a politician was deciding what I liked and telling me I was going to like it.

I was about to head to the salt mine, when the phone rang. "Mr. Boss, sir, this is Margaret McFeen, James wife. He's hurt or something, but he won't go to the emergency place. I don't know what to do, he said call you."

"What happened?" I asked.

"He was out in the barn tinkering with that contraption he's working on when it blowed-up or something. I look out; there was green smoke everywhere and he come to the house with burns on his face and hands, but he says he's all right, but said call you." Margaret began crying.

"I'll be there as soon as I can; it'll take me a while, its twenty miles to your place from mine. Stay calm, I'm on my way."

A trip to James's place was kind of an adventure in itself. You took a paved road west out of town until the pavement run out, you followed the dirt road until you ran out of county road and civilization, opened a gate, followed the cow trail through the Oak trees, at last a clearing. What came next? 'James' Place,' was hard to explain. There was the windmill collection, made out of everything from fifty five gallon drums, buckets, tin cans, air plane propellers, and things beyond identification. All doing their thing, they pumped water, made electricity, charged batteries, ran compressors for refrigeration, and Lord only knows what else.

Then there was the antenna collection, yaggie, whips, long lines, bed springs, and things, all had a wire or wires going to the barn. Then there was the barn, what once was suitable for cows, pigs and chickens, now housed the biggest array devices of unknown use, I have ever seen. Here lights, there lights, everywhere blinking lights.

"Where did you get all that stuff?" I asked James the first time I saw it.

"Made most of it" said he.

"What's it do?" I said, seeing, was not believing.

"Need for work on anti-gravitron. Think I got it figured out" said he.

"James" I said, at last "you invited me out here, what can I do? It looks to me like you don't need help, at least not my help. You left me at the starting line, in a cloud of dust."

"Got new Helix Arc machine, maybe you can 'learn' me

to run it" James said, "Need to weld new metal."

"Wanna see new Helix Arc machine?" James asked. "They said at the factory, you could weld gum wrappers together."

"James," I said, "There's just not much demand for welding gum wrappers." "What you wanting to weld, and why?" I reluctantly asked.

"New gravitation metal, I made, don't know what to call it for anti-gravitron. You show me how to run Helix Arc, sometime."

"James," I said at last, "I should be taking lessons not giving them."

"We trade," James said, "I learn about Helix Arc and stuff you know about, and I'll learn you anti-gravitron stuff, OK?"

What in this world had I agreed to?

This first visit to 'James' Place' took place shortly after James had told me the Big Bang was wrong, and that an anti-gravitron would work, and did work. Was I about to get an eye full of cider?

"I'd like to see what you're doing" I said. "Maybe you'll show me sometime."

Nobody ever wanted to see anti-gravitron before. "I'll show yous one someday soon," says James, "Youse can come out next Saturday. Iff'in yous wants to see whats I'm doin'."

<><><><><>

This time was different; an air of emergency was in Margaret's voice. Had James self-destructed I wondered.

James had built his bride a small frame house. I had never been inside. I didn't know what to expect. Mostly run of the mill except for the books everywhere, from what I could see, mostly tech manuals, and science books. There was quite a collection.

There was a number of "How To" books, on all kinds of subjects. If he had read all that stuff, and understood it, he must be a walking encyclopedia of fifty volumes. Now that I think about it, he was.

James was sitting on the couch, obviously in pain, his face and hands with obvious burns. "James" I said, "You need to go to the emergency room so they can fix you up."

"Scared never been to doctor. What they do to you?" he asked.

"I'll take you, if you'll go" I encouraged him.

"I'll go if you says I's needs to. Scared," says James.

"Can I go? I want to be with him," says Margaret.

This set of events caught me flat footed, how could a man know about the Big Bang, and not know about doctors, and Margaret asked to go.

"Can I go with you?" she asked James.

"If Boss says it's OK," James said.

On the way into town, I said "James, what happened out there?"

"Controls didn't work on anti-gravitron, it took off, won't come back," He paused, "have to start over."

"Tell me what went wrong," I said.

"Anti-gravitron, like Hysteresis drive frequency of AC alters speed modulation, didn't work right, ran away."

"Uh-Hu" I said. "You mean gravity has frequency, a wave length, like radio, or light, or gamma rays?" I asked.

"Something like that, but different" James said, matter of factly.

James was like a spy glass, look through the lenses one way, everything is bigger, but the other way everything was smaller. I never knew for sure if I saw James through the big end, or little end.

"James" I said, "This is beyond me. This is like a car; you don't have to know how a motor works to drive it. Are you telling me the motor for the contraption you built works, but the steering wheel don't?"

"Uh, that's about it" James said, then added "frequency wrong."

"What does frequency have to do with gravity?" was that the proper question I wondered.

"Nothing" James said, "Frequency for controls, not for anti-gravitron."

"Burns hurt, controls don't work." James murmured.

In the emergency room the plot thickened, the Doctor asked, "How'd you get a burn like that? It looks like sunburn, but it would take hours of intent sunlight to get a burn like that. Have you been in the sun?"

"In barn," says James.

"What happened?" the doctor asked.

"Controls don't work on anti-gravitron, it took off, won't come back, said James. "Have to start over."

"Then you was working in the barn on something, what happened?" the doctor asked.

"Controls don't work ---

The doctor interrupted, "What was you working on?"

"Anti-gravitron" James said.

"Anti-gravitron, I don't know what an anti-gravitron is." "What's an anti-gravitron?" the doctor asked.

"Motor runs on gravity, controls don't work."

"OK" said the doctor, "but what happened?"

James looked confused, and then said, "anti-gravitron left, green smoke, hurt, controls don't work." He paused, "ask Boss". He gestured toward me.

"Is Boss your name or occupation?" the doctor asked.

"For James, both and neither at the same time, maybe a more accurate term for me is language translator."

"James knows exactly what he is doing, and trying to say, but his words come out wrong. In short, he knows but can't say the words. He sees, he understands, but can't tell you about it."

"Then, do you know what happened?" the doctor asked.

"Not exactly" I said, "But I could probably guess. I haven't been out to his barn lately, but I do know what he's been messing with. His wife said there was green smoke. Green smoke tells me he was experimenting with Argon gas. That's a cover agent used in TIG, MIG, and Heli Arc welders. He has a Heli Arc welder that he has been experimenting with. I helped him set it up, and gave him a few lessons in welding, but I don't know what he was trying to weld."

I offered "The only thing I know of that burns like that is Zeta Particle Radiation, if it is, he's onto something."

"You had medical training?" the doctor asked.

"No," I said, "But I know about Zeta Particle Radiation. So does he, it can be terminal."

"Control don't work" James said again.

"Doctor," I said, "can you look at the retina of his eyes, see if it looks normal."

"What am I looking for, you seem to know something I don't'" the doctor asked.

"Anything, anything at all that's different, anything?" I begged.

"Looks normal to me" the doctor said.

CHAPTER NINE
JACK IS GONE

I had called 'Soup' and told him I'd be a little late for work, James McFeen wife called and said he's hurt. I'm going to see about him.

"Keep me posted," 'Soup' said. "I knew it wouldn't be long until he self-destructed. I guess you know he's an aspiring Space Cadet. You missed the real excitement, Sonny made an appearance; he fired Jack and made Roger Rabbit Plant Manager."

"What did you say to me? Did I hear Sonny fired Jack? And made Roger the Tattle Tale Rabbit, Plant Manager? Is this one of your or Jack's bad jokes?" I asked.

"I wish it was" said 'Soup', "There's more, talk to you later, if I'm here. See about James, I've known that basket case all his life, his mother is my sister. I knew he needed you. We were right."

That was just a lot more information than I needed in one day, Lord no more surprises today, I prayed. But the day wasn't over yet. Maybe I was fired too; I didn't have a time card. For seven years I had a time card, I had one yesterday, why not today?" I wondered to myself.

"You don't have one." 'Soup' said, "Let's have a talk, there's news, first things first, how's James?"

"He'll be back in a couple of days the doctor said, they were first and second degree burns. He had on eye protection, he'll lose some hide, but it'll grow back. He'll still be ugly and lost," I said.

"His eyes, did they look at his eyes?" 'Soup' seemed to be concerned.

"Uh, yes, I insisted they look at his eyes retina, the doctor said all looked normal." I said. 'Soup' looked relieved.

"Zeta Particle Radiation, maybe?" 'Soup asked.

Stunned, I stammered, "Maybe. You know about Zeta Particles?"

"You're not the only one who has been around exotic flying machines. I cut my teeth on U-Twos. Now, are your ears ready for saucy bits of information? It's been a long, long day. Mine will end real quick, it won't take me long to hit the high points. You'll figure out the rest," 'Soup' continued.

"The war started a little after eight this morning, Sonny and the General Secretary showed up about nine or so from Chicago, 'for consultation' says they. I was invited. Sonny laid out the new plan, Jack, went through the roof. 'You're an idiot,' was Jack's appraisal of the situation.

"Like the fly on the wall that I was and aim to be, I gathered that Roger Rabbit had convinced Sonny that the high production totals was his doing. He ordered the production quotas, that's all there was to it.

"Jack pointed out to them that the reason the production was way up, was because a bunch of hard working capable people made the quota possible. And then added, that if you two idiots think all you have to do to up production is order it done, you're even bigger idiots that I think you are. That did it, Jack cleaned out his office, and Sonny announced, that Roger the

Snitch Rabbit was now Plant Manager.

"Tomorrow morning at nine AM, I am to be in the Rabbit's new office, for my new marching orders. The world answers to the Rabbit, and he only answers to Sonny. It'll be clear as mud, by noon tomorrow!

"Oh, by the way, I hear you are the Maintenance Soup now, he smiled that having fun grin. Congratulations!

"Moñana, a new day dawns in never, never land! I'm a year or so away from retirement; I gotta hang on if I can. With Jack gone and those imbecile's are now in charge. I see bad days ahead. That half-wit shot himself in the foot, probably both feet, and don't know how much it's going to hurt. See you tomorrow, maybe," he said as he left.

I didn't know what happened to my time card, when did I become management? Or was I out of a job? 'Soup' said I had a new job, I was absolutely certain; I did NOT want a new job! Nor did I want to be Maintenance Superintendent. I had the best job in the Plant, with the best men to work with, nor did I have any patients with politics. I build things; fix things, make things work, that's all, at the end of my shift I just want to go home. Home is where your heart is, and my heart was with the house I had been working on for four years.

CHAPTER TEN
THE VOTE

I was able to buy a small acreage out of town, and was building a home for my growing family, a dream home, a high efficiency solar home of my own design. Factory paychecks, now bought boards, concrete and nails, in my racing days in bought car parts. Eight AM to One PM, belonged to me and home construction. Two PM to Ten PM belonged to the Factory, I wasn't looking for a schedule change on my part, nor did I get a vote.

My vote is the one that is going to count, I haven't decided yet. After talking to 'Soup', I didn't know whether to stay or go home. I went to the electric shop, to hide from the day and the collection of crazies. I wanted to be left alone and think, especially to be left alone.

The first to appear to disrupt my own personal revolt was Robert Green, "Margaret called her mama, said James got hurt and you took him to the ER. How bad is he hurt?"

"Not too bad," I said. "The doctor said he'd be alright in a few days."

"Thanks for seeing to him and Margaret," he added. "I don't think James could live without you. You two speak a language that no one else understands, at least I don't. If he talks at all, it's about stuff I know nothing about, or about Boss, or about anti-gravitrons, or saucers.

"Margaret says he's the gentlest person, but can't say things the right way. He just shows her. That's, as you know, how he is. He can't tell you, he just gets the job done. I think the world of him as odd as he is. Thanks," Robert said, "Thanks again."

Robert turned about to leave, took a few steps; turned back to face me, "Rumor has it that big changes are afoot. Thanks again for looking out for James, and the rest of us Misfits."

"James is my friend, so are you and, and – GIT," I said, was I going to unravel?

Thankfully I got to go home at a decent hour; my wife was still up when I got home. "You can't believe what kind of a day I've had." I said, as I slumped down in my chair. "Dear it's late but we need to talk, I – We got to make some tough decisions, my world got turned upside down." I hit the highpoints, as best I could, knowing only what 'Soup' had said.

"What do you want to do?" she asked.

"I don't know. If –When I lose this job, I think I'll try it on my own; twenty years of factory work is enough. Work awhile, make plans for a future, then 'Poof' out of a job and you have to start over. I'm tired of starting over. I'm tired of working for idiots; with 'Soup' and Jack it was different. But Sonny and Roger No-account, is the last straw. What is real important to me now is my men, they made me look good, they made 'Soup' look good, they made Jack look good; they made the plant look good, even Roger looked good. Jack knew the truth, 'Soup' knew the truth, and I most assuredly know the truth, my men deserve a lot better than they are going to get now.

These years at the factory were mostly my new race car. I knew when I had done my best. It was honest, no excuses, do your best no excuses, next time learn from your mistakes, build a better car, and learn to drive better, no excuses. When the time comes, you have nothing left to prove, hang up your helmet, no regrets, no excuses, and no apologies. Being a has been is better than a never was. I am a, has been, not a never was.

"Well, I know you," she said. "I know this house is not quite done, it would be nice if it was finished before you become another has been. We kept eating when we were in college and having kids, we kept eating when your mother died, we kept eating in car racing and in factory work. We couldn't leave when we got out of college, now we have roots, we can't leave now. Do what you must, we'll keep eating. Oh, how's James? Somebody called from the Plant looking for you. They wanted to know if you were back from the ER yet. I freaked out; I thought it was you again. Then they assured me it was not you, it was James. Sometimes I think he should be one of your children."

<><><><><>

The next morning, my wife was off to work, and our kids to school, and I was still seething about the events of yesterday. I knew I had to decide what I intended to do, I just knew it was bad news, when the phone rang. "Mr. Carter, the new Plant Manager has called a staff meeting in the Conference Room at ten o'clock this morning. All staff is required to attend," the secretary said.

This is just no way to run a railroad, I said to myself. This is not in my plan, my plan is to go work at two o'clock and work until ten and go home. Staff hours are eight till four. I definitely don't want to work eight to four.

I arrived at the conference a few minutes early and sat down by 'Soup'. "If I got a call to attend a staff meeting, does this mean I'm now staff?" I smiled.

"You're the new Soup" 'Soup' said.

"You want to bet?" I said.

"This should be an interesting meeting," 'Soup' said, smiling.

Roger the Rabbit Carter, our new Plant Manager, entered the conference all smiles. "As you all know by now; substantial new changes are taking place. As the new Plant Manager, I have been instructed by the CEO at Corporate headquarters, to enact a new operational plan. As you know the CEO has authorized construction of six new production lines in a new addition. We will soon be streamlining our operation protocol. I am honored to announce, two new staff members positions as well as personnel reassignments. Herb, formerly Head Electrician, will now assume the position of Chief of Computer Operations, with the responsibility of upgrading all computer operations, our long time Maintenance Superintendent affectionately known as 'Soup' will assume the office as Liaison to Engineering to the Corporate HQ, the former Second Shift Maintenance Foreman known as unofficial head of the Misfits will assume the position as New Superintendent of Maintenance, as well as Chief of Construction on the new production lines, and Robert Green second shift mechanic will be the New Second Shift Maintenance Foreman.

"There is now a vacancy for Head Electrician, with Herb's promotion. Other changes will soon be announced. That about covers it for today, as a new administrative policy there will be a general staff meeting every Monday at Ten AM, attendance for all staff will be mandatory. Have we any questions before we adjourn?"

I raised by hand like a school boy, "Yoo-hoo," I waved my hand and hollered "Yoo-hoo! I don't want to rain on your parade; however I feel I must point out a slight problem in this new way of doing things." I said.

"What is wrong with the new agenda, Chicago authorized it." Roger the Rabbit said.

"The biggest problem I see at this time is," I paused, "I don't intend to be the New Maintenance Soup, nor do I have any desire to work new hours." I added, "Sorry if this upsets your apple cart. That's all I have to say."

The ashen color of Roger the Rabbit Carter's face turned a glowing red, he stammered in unbelief, "You mean to say that you don't intend to accept this new promotion?"

"Yep" I said, "That's what I said, nor do I have any desire to change my working hours. By the way, my time card vanished yesterday."

"Staff are salaried, they don't need time cards. You sure you won't accept a promotion or a raise?"

"Yup, that's what I said, uh, can I go now, I don't belong in a staff meeting?" I asked.

"Misfit certainly suits you well." The rabbit snarled as I walked out.

CHAPTER ELEVEN

GRAVITRON

I had a couple of hours left after I walked out of the meeting. I drove out to 'James's Place', to see how he was doing. As I got out of the truck, Margaret hollered from the house, "He's in here, we're reading a book."

Did she say, we're reading a book? As I enter James's house, he was sitting on the couch, with his hands in the air, with a book opened on his lap, he gave a slight smile amid the blister's and scars on his face.

"How ya doin'?" I asked.

"Frequency modulator theory book" James said.

"James," I asked, "What happened out there yesterday?"

"Controls don't work on anti-gravitron, need to start over. We go to barn, I show you, new machine. Made new anti-gravitron. Controls don't work." James said.

We walked the hundred yards or so to the barn. I had been there before. Sometime back I had given James some lessons in using the new Heli Arc machine.

"James," I said, "What are you wanting to weld anyway?"

"Don't know what to call it," says he, "I'll show you

some."

James gestured toward a piece of what I thought was aluminum foil. It was about six inches square and as thin as a piece of paper. So this was the gum wrapper he wanted to weld together, but why? I picked up the piece of foil, James said, "I made anti-gravitron material. You bend." said James, "You bend."

I may be a city boy now, but I haven't always been. I milked a lot of cows out on the farm and have what I believed, better than average, upper body strength. That is a plus driving short track dirt cars.

Stunned, I could not bend it, even slightly! "James," I said, "what in the name of God is this?"

"Anti-gravitron metal, I made," says he.

"Uh...uh...uh...how?... How'd you do that? It looks like aluminum foil" I said, unbelievingly.

"It was," says he, "Changed to anti-gravitron material." "I show you new machine. Make anti-gravitron material," says he.

James gestured to a box of aluminum foil; I pulled out about six inches, folded it, and then tore it in half. I took it to a nearby table to what looked like a microwave oven. I placed the foil in the 'Machine' as instructed. "Watch," says he.

I turn what obviously was a control pot switch. A hum like you hear when you use your home microwave. Astonished, I saw the aluminum foil rise to the center of the machine, a faint green glow began to appear as the aluminum arose to the center of the microwave. It just levitated there, in the center of the machine with that green glow. After a minute or so, the machine quit humming, gently the aluminum foil settled back down.

James said "Open door of the machine, and take out the foil. Not hot," says he, "anti-gravitron material."

What a few minutes ago was tin foil now was something I could not bend. I just stood there – foil in hand - staring at James! Not really believing what I had just seen and done. "James, can you explain what I have just seen?" I asked staring at him in disbelief.

"No," says he, "got no words" he paused, and softly said, "I know, got no words." James seemed to be lost, going somewhere. Then added, "You Boss, know lots stuff, you say words."

"James" I said, "I don't have the foggiest idea what I have just seen. How – how can I explain it?"

"I find way, I show you, you say words," says he.

CHAPTER TWELVE
MOHAMMAD

Maybe I should have paid more attention in "Magnet 101" I have known how to levitate aluminum since I was a kid in the sixth grade. A traveling 'Science Guy' came to our school and gave a demonstration of science machines and how they work, like Van DeGriff Generators that makes your hair stand on end with static electricity. And strong electromagnets arranged in an order when turned on makes an aluminum pan levitate. Such devises are called repulsion coils.

I thought levitating aluminum was a neat trick, so a few years later I built my version of a repulsion coil, and Van DeGriff Generator. I entered them in the science fair. I was second place in the local, but got beat out by my buddy that made a photo cell in his dad's garage. His research was better, my show was better. He won, I learned a lesson, and so did he I think. Show and know is a hard act to follow.

As a rather successful racecar driver over a number of years, I learned early in my racing career the value of a good show. It keeps fans coming, fans mean money, and money means regular meals and a new car for next season.

What keeps you racing is respect, nothing else. Car racing is a violent sport. There is an unwritten law of kill or be killed at times. The idea and reality of payback is what earns respect.

It is not for the timid. It's like getting shot in combat, the guy shooting at you is not mad, he's not scared, he's just doing his job. You'd better be better or maybe luckier than he is. There is a real difference in taking a chance and taking a calculated risk.

Most people, at least a lot of them, never put their life on the starting line for a cause even once. But, I did one or two or three times a week, in racing season for years, and being shot at is a mind expanding experience.

There is a real difference between combat and car racing. In combat you are facing someone you don't know. What you know least about scares you the most. But in car racing you know who and what you are up against. After a while you know your rivals better than they know themselves, it keeps you alive sometimes.

I left James at 'James' Place' and drove back to the salt mine. I remembered those conversations we had over the last six years or so, it wasn't my technical knowledge, it was my courage or maybe my demonstrated tenacity to function at a high level when a real level of personal danger existed. The reality of what I now knew about James scared me to death.

James had somehow figured out something no human being on earth knew, but was unable to tell someone. He wanted me, his friend to 'say words' how could I say words about something I couldn't describe. James was onto something, something incredible, and had to see it through, to its end. He was building a flying saucer, and intended to fly it. No one else on earth could do it. How such a thing could be done, only James knew.

When I got to the factory, I entered the south door, as I had for seven years. But this time was a bit different, would I have a time card, or be out of a job. 'Soup' met me with that characteristic 'have fun at my expense' smile.

"Here's your time card." 'Soup' handed me my time card,

"You sure got the old pot boiling today, he smiled, "You managed to get fired, hired, promoted and demoted all in a matter of a few minutes. Now the steam is coming out of the Rabbits big ears. He had it all planned out, and you single handedly made a mess of everything. He wants you gone, but Chicago wants you to build the new production lines, and Roger the Prize is in a little jam. THIS," said 'Soup' "is going to be fun to watch!"

After you broke up the meeting and upset Roger's apple-cart, I figured you went to see about James. How's my nephew doing anyway?" 'Soup' asked. "I hear he's made a new machine. Did you see it? Were you impressed?" 'Soup' smiled again.

"You know about that barn out there and what he's doing?" somewhat surprised I asked.

"Of course." said 'Soup' "He's my nephew; I've known him all his life, we learned years ago to just let him be. That's about the only thing you could do with him. Everybody in our family recognized early in his life, that he had a special gift. By three or four he'd take a clock apart and put it back together. By the time he started school he was taking the radio apart. In school, he just wasn't like other kids when he learned to read, Dick and Jane just didn't interest him, Edison did. How long was it before you knew he couldn't write?" 'Soup' asked.

"A day or two after you sent him my way." I said, "I had seen a couple of such folks in combat usually after they had seen their best buddy vanish before their eyes. Something set them off to a different world, but you say James has always been that way." I asked. "Can I ask you a personal question, why did you hire James when you did?"

"I was waiting for somebody like you. I knew James could fix a machine with the best of them, but you have to let him be. Here's the thing, when I saw you're name on that job application, I knew who you were by reputation. I had been around the race track to hear and see your escapades and this old man I go to church with, he and I have been best of friends since high school. He was some kind of foreman at that plant across town that folded up sometime ago; anyway, he said they had a Misfit over there that could fix anything. And if he couldn't fix it, he would make you a new one. But, you just had to leave him alone. Point him at it, and get out of the way, is the way Sam Johnson put it."

"We traded insults a few times." I said. "He seemed to think I could drive three wheel cars, better than four wheel ones."

'Soup' continued, "When it looked like you might stay after your mother died, we thought it might be a good time to try James. As far as we knew, James had never run into another Whizz Kid, Misfit, and an older one at that. What did we have to lose? Things were in a mess anyway. Within a week of your arrival we began to hope, the new kid would amount to something. The down time went down and production went up on third shift. We thought it might be a good time to see if you and James could work together. When you and James hit it off, history was in the making."

"Well just exactly who is 'We'? You and the mouse in your pocket?" I snarled.

"Why no," 'Soup' smiled that grin again, "Jack, my sister's and me, is 'We'."

"What's Jack got to do with James?" I asked, confused.

"It's simple; Jack is married to my other sister. You and James both live in a vacuum, in outer space." There was that all knowing smile again.

"I'm wondering now, how I could work here seven years and not know you and Jack were brother-in-laws," I, in my stupidity, asked.

'Soup' was really enjoying himself at my expense, there was that smile. "That's easy to answer too, if you want to know something, you got to ask the right question. If it's about people, you talk people talk. If you want to know anything about machines, you ask a machine who can talk."

"My job is translator; I talk people talk and machine talk. The real problem around here is you and James speaks some kind of alien dialect. When something needs explaining to the Muckity Mucks, they talk to me in people, I talk to you in machine talk, and you talk to James in alien, now isn't that simple?" 'Soup' was smiling again.

"Now here's what went wrong in this fool's paradise of never, never land. Big Boss knew how factories work. Big Boss was a very wise man, when he found a golden goose that laid golden eggs, he wasn't about to kill her. Big Boss collected golden eggs, but Big Boss got old, got sick and died. Now Sonny inherited the golden eggs, now being a half-witted gander, he never laid an egg in his life. He had no idea that only golden geese lay golden eggs. Then comes Roger Tattle Tale, he comes out from under his rock and tells Sonny that golden eggs come from the Easter Bunny. Now Jack tries to tell Sonny and Roger Half-wit the facts in factory life. Now Sonny the real intellect runs Jack out of town. Sonny and Roger the Rabbit devise a new plan of action. Now here's the fun part,"

'Soup continued, "Now Big Boss liked golden eggs, and this plant became his best layer, Big Boss swoops down here for a look see, likes what he sees, and tells Jack to see to the new program. Now Jack is the most capable administrator I've ever known, or heard tell of. He knows everybody, what they can do and lets them do it. His ability to put the right people in the right place is uncanny. That collection of Misfits was no accident; it produced remarkable results in a short time. Big Boss's motto was don't fix what ain't broke, that was Jack's and that's mine as well. Now you Misfits are a different breed, your motto should be as long as it runs well, leave it alone, hoping it breaks so you can fix it better, and make it run longer and faster. That's the real golden eggs."

"And then Mohammad announced, 'me no move' I personally am just dying to see the mountains move. Jack knew exactly what would happen if they messed with what made everybody look good, and told them so. I told them what would happen. The chickens came home to roost, when you told them. Now the Fox is in charge of the chicken coop. OH! By the way," 'Soup' smiled, "the first moving mountain produced you a new time card."

CHAPTER THIRTEEN
NO MORE

Things around the salt mine settled down somewhat. 'Soup' as far as I was concerned, was still 'Soup'. And I was still officially Second Shift Maintenance Foreman. I still had a job to do. James was back, everybody and I mean everybody in the Misfit world missed James. Over the last seven years or so he had become an integral part of Misfit livelihood. In spite of his peculiarities he was one of us, a real cog in our wheel. Without him things were just not as smooth operating.

In the seven years James had been here, he had never missed a day of work, was never late. He took one week of vacation to get married about three years ago. That's about the time my real vocation changed from car racing to house building.

When I first took my car racing serious, I ran a gas station. Pay checks, bought food, paid the rent and bought car parts. Winnings, if and when, were part pay check. When they passed the G.I. Bill about ten years after I got out of service, I went back to school. Now I was one of the old vets on campus. The Vietnam war was winding down, and there was a G.I. Bill. A lot of veterans went and enlisted in the college wars of education.

No more factory work, no more gas stations, no more electrical work. Just No More! Nothing, except race cars, books, maybe eventual law school. Anyway I had a real advantage; I had a real high tech skill and experience, whether I went to college or not. I could support a new wife and family without a college degree. But I wanted one and was willing to pay the price to get one, nor did I have to cheat to get a degree. I did my own homework and got a lot better education than I had before college.

I graduated with a Pre Law Degree, with lots of History and Government classes. But for electives I took physics, chemistry, biology, zoology, math and architecture. No basket weaving, P.E., or bowling. For entertainment a few high speed laps around the race track was relaxing, at least for me. It was kind of like getting shot at, it keeps your mind off unimportant things.

Not long after my mother died, my wife and I bought a small acreage outside of town. In short order, I began work on the new house. Like some young men do, I bought an old house and remodeled it in my spare time while my family and I lived in saw dust. That's just not a lifestyle everyone could endure, but poor folks have poor ways. Coming from the sticks where I come from, until I was adopted at twelve years old. Poor was a way of life I didn't know there was anything else. Poor farm, with poor dirt, produced poor folks. But, with adoption, poor was no more. Rich now, was three meals a day, a warm bed in a warm house, a T.V. to watch and a car that would run without some praying and tinkering. That, where I came from, was rich. More than that for me was unnecessary, just luxury. Now rich I was able to go to school all day, every day. I had lunch money and a quarter to buy a motor with. For me, life just don't get any better than that. Now I could dare to dream the big dream. In short order after becoming rich at twelve, fame came next, recognition for achievements, and pats on the back for good deeds was far better than ridicule, and no lunch money and positively no motor to mess with.

For me I learned early in life the merits of superior 'learning' and hard work. Success breeds more success. Poor breeds more poor. When your outlook on life changes, no matter why, your life changes. That change in my life triggered an upward spiral, from poor to rich, from nobody to somebody, from homeless to a cutting edge solar energy home, of my own design, built in my spare time. What next for me, earth bound to flying saucers? Thanks to James and his dedication to an idea and a cause that makes no sense, whatsoever, to the masses of humanity. I have found myself teetering on the edge of the unknown, the one thing I fear.

James was onto something but could not tell anyone about it, but, could demonstrate a profound and superior knowledge. I have been reminded of an adage my grandpa used to tell me when as a kid questions came up, when I lived on the farm. Grandpa would say, "Boy, things don't just happen. Go out in the bushes, find a tree stump, and sit there until you figure it out. It'll come to you if you sit there long enough."

James had sat on his tree stump and figured it out, but what language did he think in? I think in English, my ideas, concepts and realities are verbalized in English. Language fails us when in complex and traumatic situations. We stutter, we stammer, we babble, when we can't explain things nor can we write. James's haunting words came back to me, "I find way, you say words."

Jack had been gone four or five months. I really missed his stupid jokes. I missed his noisy surprise visits, in short, I missed Jack. I had known for some time that Jack and 'Soup' were my guardian angels, and I had no doubt who made me what I was around the factory. The debt I owed them was un-payable, they were my protectors, my companions, and my comrades in arms, and they gave be the chance to work and do my best.

A good definition of a good friend was someone who looked right through you and was not disturbed by the view.

Nothing I saw in Jack disturbed me, nothing I saw in 'Soup' disturbed me, and nothing I saw in James disturbed me, except James's preoccupation and dedication to anti gravitrons, whatever that really meant. Anti gravitrons were more than motors that runs on gravity.

'Soup' met me at the time clock. The new Plant Manager avoided me like the plague. Occasionally he would send one of his 'yes' men to 'feel me out', about what I thought about some trivial something, anything important came from 'Soup'. "Let's go have a little chat," 'Soup' grinned, "The Mountains are really moving now."

It seems somebody somewhere has rethought the unthinkable. It seems that Roger the Dodger has dodged the silver bullet for the time being. He's still in charge of the plant. However maintenance and construction are to remain a maintenance problem. Rumor has it that production might be better off considering, what maintenance thought about machine operations, like in the old days. In the old days, about all Chicago knew or wanted to know was what they read in a report, numbers like golden eggs in and golden eggs out, if Big Boss added to his golden egg collection everything was fine, Jack got to go play golf and learn some more stupid jokes.

If a problem arose, Jack would go talk to the proper person who could solve the problem. Usually he would tell one of his stupid jokes, and tell them what the problem was, and usually that was that. If things went as planned, next time it was only a stupid joke. He knew who to trust and who not to trust.

If a machine problem came up, he'd talk to me, or one of the mechanic foremen, depending on the problem, the same thing with production.

"Oh," said 'Soup', "did you know that Jack and I both came up through the ranks as line mechanics in this plant?"

"No," I said, "you said I lived in a vacuum, I guess you were right, maybe I do need to learn people talk!"

That smile again, "Probably not possible," 'Soup' said, "house and alien suits you better. Seen the saucer lately?" 'Soup' smiled that smile again, "Chicago sent these blueprints and proposal down here for a 'look see', maybe you and a Misfit or two could look them over and see what is wrong with them. I'll have to write the report. As far as I know none of you Misfits can write. They decided I need a plant engineer around here to build that new addition, if you're interested, I voted for you."

"I'll think about it, if it's two to ten." I said.

"Do you think James can make it as an electrician if he works for you?"

"I'll ask him." I smiled.

"You know I might make it to retirement yet!" 'Soup' said.

I took a few minutes and looked through the stack of blueprints, and proposals on 'Soup's' piled up table. Enough junk had been moved around so you could unfold the blueprints.

I started back down to the electric shop, one of the Misfits met me at the door, both hands on his hips with a look of sheer disgust on his face, and in a loud voice announced, "It's about time you showed up, you're getting to be a real Boss now. You're never around when somebody needs you, and now when nobody wants you, or needs you, you show up."

While I am being severely chastised, and abused, Robert and James decided to join the fun. "All right," I said, "Now you've done it, you've hurt my feelings. So I'll tell you what I'm going to do, I'm going to stay down here and mind the store, and cry my eyes out, while you three – uh, uh, Misfits trot your butt's down to 'Soup's' office and take a peek at that pile of blueprints and proposals, at least you can look at the pictures.

James, look at those schematics, and energy requirements, see how they line up with their proposals. Robert see if the machine locations will do what they want them to do, and you eloquent one, if you still remember anything whatsoever about plumbing, or pipefitting, at least look at the pictures.

"Oh," said the eloquent one "I still know the only two rules in plumbing and pipefitting. Number one, Do-Do always runs downhill, and Number two, keep your mouth shut when you're around Boss's and open sewage lines. They're about the same."

"I've had all of this I can stand," I said in my most pathetic voice, "Now GIT before I start my Boo-Hoo." All three took off in a make believe trot toward 'Soup's' office.

For a few days, the natives were rather quiet, it was a good time to talk to James. "You had enough time to look those blueprints and proposals over?" I asked James.

"Uh, yes'ser, I see'd `em," says he.

"What'd you think of them" I asked.

"Is that what blueprints and proposal look like," says James.

"That's about it," I said. "You catch on what they are about?" I asked.

"Uh, yes'ser," says he, "not like anti-gravitron, and modulator stuff." A long searching pause, "proposals meet parameters."

"Parameters? I said, Parameters, did I hear you say parameters?"

"Uh, yes'ser," says he "Learn meaning of new word.

Parameter, Margaret helped me look up word in Dick – dictionary! Got new big dick – dic – dictionary, I learn new word draw
circle around it. Learn meaning, new word, draw circle, not say,
draw circle."

I must have looked as confused as I was stunned; all I
could say was "Uh-Hu"

Then James added, "You Boss, you say words. I draw circle
in books, in dictionary too."

James had caught me unprepared, and unable to engage
him in an intelligent conversation, more than once. This was
one of those times.

"Uh, James, I guess you have heard there are some changes
going on around here?" I said.

"Uncle Jack, go home, Uncle 'Soup' retire soon, you go
build house soon. No Boss, not stay," says he.

"That's about right," I said, "but the not stay is what I
want to talk about." "James, you know Herb is moving to the
front office, that leaves an opening for an electrician, on second
shift. You're the best candidate I know of that can do that job."

"You boss, I like, work for you, scared." James said.

"James," I said, "You and I have worked together for the
last seven years or so, and you have been the second shift electrician for the last five years, whether you know it or not, and
the third shift electrician for the year before that. James, I know
you can do the work. James," I said, "at least think about this,
talk to Margaret, talk to Uncle Jack, talk to 'Soup', talk to Robert, those folks know you better than I do."

I don't know how much of this got through to him, I
never knew. I just explained the problem as I saw it and stand
back and let him solve it. James stood there a few moments
looking that bewildered lost look, at last, says he "You Boss, talk

to you, talk to Margaret. Like you, like Margaret," says he.

At last, I asked, "How's the new machine coming along?"

"Make new anti-gravitron, maybe controls work, want to see?" James asked.

"You bet" I said, "Saturday maybe?"

"Saturday, you come, new big anti-gravitron, new controls, anti-gravitron stay this time." James smiled.

CHAPTER FOURTEEN
THING

I hadn't been out to 'James' Place' since his accident. I was now spending more time on my home construction project. I could see an end to my home project. The idea of starting my own business in the foreseeable future was a real possibility. I had done my homework and I was sure I had a good chance of success.

Anyway, one way or another, I would probably leave the factory. If Roger the Dodger Rabbit remained Plant Manager, I would probably leave in a huff. Whether I waited long enough to build the new edition, was the question. Money had never been my motivation in car racing, nor was in it the solar high efficiency home building. It was, I guess, ego. I just wanted to be able to run with a fast crowd, and be able to hold my own with the best there was in the world I lived in. Most people never want to take on the big dogs on their own turf; most folks are never able to run with big dogs, they prefer to lie on the porch. I just never could understand that. There is just something to be said about being really good at something. Good enough to win without cheating.

James is a big dog, he don't even know there is a porch to lie on. This saucer thing is honest work, harder work than most folks, including me, are willing to endure. What makes it even more remarkable, is his obvious handicap. What concerns me about James and his anti-gravitron is something I know a lot about. I was able to stay alive by knowing the real difference between calculated risk and chance. When risk becomes chance, the odds are overwhelming against you. It's like buying a lottery ticket.

With the anti-gravitron thing, I am not certain; the question of risk or chance has any meaning with James. Anti-gravitron, for James is just a problem, to solve. It's just that simple, but chance and odds have real consequences.

As I got out of my truck, on Saturday, Margaret gestured toward the barn. "He out there with that thing."

'Thing', she called it. That might be more understandable than anti-gravitron or anti-gravitation machine. Whatever it was, it was beginning to tickle my curiosity cells. As I neared the barn, James came out smiling.

"Got big anti-gravitron, controls work, needs house now. Come in barn, I show you." James said, just beaming.

I had never in the eight years I had known James seen him so animated. "I show you new big anti-gravitron. Controls work, Need house," says he.

Around James' barn, at 'James' Place', I knew very well to expect the unforeseeable, I was right, 'Thing' was the absolute best definition possible for the new machine.

There in the middle of the barn floor – was – whatever it was. I'll try to describe the 'thing'. Visualize a kids wading pool, the kind you pump up. About ten feet across and a foot high with a row of soda cans all around the inside parameter, next there is a folding lawn chair, setting in the middle of the shiny pool 'thing'. There is a cube about a foot square, or so, under the lawn chair and what resembled an old truck gear stick shifter in front of the lawn chair.

"Put on glasses. I show how anti-gravitron works. I make house next," says he. James handed me a pair of goggles, with blue lenses, to put on. And he put on a similar pair. "Makes Zeta Particle," says he.

James took his seat in the lawn chair, reached down to the cube and turned a switch on, "takes a bit to warm up," says he, "controls work, now know how to make controls work better," says he.

After a minute or so, a slight hum could be heard, and a green looking glow began to illuminate the shiny wading pool, James did something with the gear shifter thing, the 'thing' began to rise from the floor.

The 'thing' moved forward, back, left, right, esque, then rotated one way, then the other, then up some more, then gently settled back down to the floor. James reached down to the cube and turned off the switch. The hum and glow subsided.

James sitting in the lawn chair announced, "need house, like airplane, I make soon."

After I was able to breathe again, I removed the goggles and just stood there, looking at the saucer, 'thing'. At last I was able to utter, "James, how you do that?"

"Made anti-gravity motor, controls in the box" say he.

"But how'd you do that?" I asked again.

"Made anti-gravity motor, controls in box, make house like airplane soon," says he.

Talking to James is like – is like – is like sitting down at a table to work a puzzle. Someone pores out a thousand pieces before you but you don't see the picture on the box. First things first find two pieces to put together, then a third. In time with lots of effort, in trial and error, eventually the puzzle picture becomes a reality. But with James you see the picture on the box, but most of the pieces are missing. Where are the missing pieces? They're not in the box. Some of the missing pieces were crucial to completing the puzzle. You look at the box and get an idea of what was missing, but don't know their shape.

There was the machine that was made of anti-gravitron metal. Nothing I knew of could take a piece of kitchen tin foil and turn it into a piece of metal, I could not bend.

"James" I said, "can I look at that machine, and maybe I can understand what makes it work".

"You look at machine. Say words," said he.

<><><><><><>

I began by looking at the machine that mad the anti-gravi-tron metal.

The mystery just deepened. I opened the door to the machine, and observed a removable glass plate, covering a glass dish full of some lightly translucent pink liquid. The vessel that held the liquid looked like something your wife bakes a cake in. covered by a pane of glass.

"What is this liquid?" I asked, "What does it have to do with turning aluminum foil into anti-gravitron metal?"

James struggled in an effort to tell me, "like soap, like water, like more soap, more water, pink dirt, yellow dirt, more soap, more water," says he.

"I get it now" I said, "that liquid, is a combination of chemicals. Then what happens?" I asked.

"Put metal in machine, turn knob," says he.

"What happens when you turn knob?" I asked.

The answer was obvious. How it did it was obvious, the

end product was obvious. What was not obvious was how the molecular structure of aluminum foil could become anti-gravitron metal.

Metal alloying, tempering, annealing, is a science developed over the centuries, from the bronze age, to the iron age, to the steel age, then the aluminum age, plutonium age is the next advance in metal science, the anti-gravitron metal?

All these advances in human endeavor can be read about in great detail in history, chemistry and physics books. Understanding comes after a great amount of knowledge on the subject. James obviously had read a lot and had come upon something beyond my understanding, of what James called anti-gravitron.

This was the car thing again, you don't have to know how a motor works, to drive a car, and it follows that the person who understands motors may not drive cars. But some of us understand how motors work and how to drive a car, too. James understands the motor, and now is planning on driving the saucer.

I must admit I have spent a lot of time on my tree stump, not only for the idiosyncrasies of solar home construction, but anti gravitrons also. After a detailed look, at the metal making machine, I could theorize what happened. Theory is always somebody's guesswork, or someone's opinion based on what may or may not be fact, and then extrapolated to a conclusion, not proven yet. And quite often wrong from the offset.

Facts however are facts, anti-gravitron metal and anti-gravitron motor is fact, not guess work. After tree stumping on anti-gravitron metal, it came to me as grandpa said that liquid in that bowl was activated by a frequency modulator. That frequency was the key. The unknown liquid was the catalyst. And the whole process took place in a strong magnetic field.

What was and is most tantalizing, is what that liquid was made up of. Only James knew, and he was unable to tell anyone. That cocktail was most likely made up of readily available chemicals around the house, or the factory, put together in amounts only James knew. As well as the frequency and the magnetic strength only James knew. James's words haunted me at times, "You Boss, I find way, you find words."

What did not fit well with what little I really knew about James' project had to do with Zeta particles. When supersonic aircraft, re-entry vehicles, and missile technology, was in its infancy, workers exposed to those crafts shortly after landing, developed a sickness that ran its course rather quickly. One of the first signs was a green cast, around the retina of the eye. A preventative cure was discovered, blue colored lens in the goggles, worn with protective clothing. You now see people retrieving re-entry machines. That has solvied the problem. The Zeta particle contamination was short lived. Within minutes, it seemed the Zeta particle was no longer a concern. Only people who have worked around supersonic vehicles had ever heard of Zeta particles. Sometimes a faint green glow was reported. How James knew of it and about blue lenses, was another mystery.

The thinking back then was, that Zeta particles had to do with the change in molecular structure at high speed in the atmosphere, maybe related to heat generated. But James' machine didn't produce heat.

CHAPTER FIFTEEN
MOVING ON

I took on the new assignment rather reluctantly, and somewhat apprehensive, knowing that I would from time to time have to be around Roger the Pest. Roger decided one day I should have an office to do my important work, besides staff men should wear a suit and tie, besides it doesn't look good for men in my position covered in dirt and grunge. I thanked him for his concern, but informed him all the office I needed was where the problem was, and that was where my important work was. Then I told him all the blueprints was down in 'Soup's' office among all that trash, besides no one around here could read any, we just looked at the pictures. That pretty well got rid of him for a while.

'Soup' came by for a little chit chat, smiling again. "Hear you and Roger now have an understanding, you are rude, arrogant, and reprehensible, and you are leader of a cult. I told him everybody around here, except him, knew that from the first day. You show up after climbing out from under your rock, I just told him the truth, he was not amused. I think he might have been annoyed.

"You're really having fun," I said, "As usual at my expense."

"We have been asked for a recommendation for new production head, I been leaning toward Richard Burns, what do you think?" 'Soup' asked.

"Richard Burns" I snarled, "A Misfit to production, with what he knows about machines, and then production, why he'll be Plant Manager in a year or two if he'd learn some stupid jokes."

"That's kinda what I was thinking" 'Soup' smiled that all knowing smile, "That's how Jack made it."

"This project is winding down pretty quick, think you'll hang around the company?" 'Soup asked.

"Probably not," I said. "My house need's me, besides Roger don't," I smiled.

"Well," 'Soup' said. "Some mention was made to me about another job up north, or maybe something down here like an engineer with a nice office to write your reports in, or maybe Plant Manager with a big office to putt golf balls in, or maybe my luxury office" 'Soup' grinned.

"You keep this up, I'll quit before I get done here. Friend, you can tell them thanks but no thanks. I'll be moving on pretty soon."

"You know they'll be pretty mad, 'bout you not moving up north, I'll not be surprised if a mountain don't come down here to get you to change your vote." 'Soup' grinned again, "Jack and I both knew you'd never make it around here."

<><><><><>

My tenure at the factory lasted about eight years, but it was time for me to move on. The next two years or so were an ordeal, for me, working for someone is a lot easier than working for yourself. But I learned years ago that the people around you will make you or break you. Jack knew that, 'Soup' knew that, and I knew that, and I most assuredly knew that now. Fortunately for me the men and women around me are making me look good. Another thing I knew is, no man is an island, and there is no man that can't be replaced given time. I've been replaced a number of times, but maybe some men are a little harder to replace, it takes a little longer sometimes, and maybe the first choice isn't the best choice. Anyway life goes on.

My hands and I was taking a lunch break, sometime back when one of the carpenters piped up, "Say did you hear about the UFO out west of town the other day?" he said, "They thought it landed out in the timber somewhere. The cops went out to investigate, said they didn't find anything."

"Oh yeah," piped up another, "Heard about that, they said there was one out north of town too, somewhere about your place," he said pointing at me. "You didn't happen to see it did you?"

"As a matter of fact I did." I said, smiling. "It landed in my yard and a spaceman got out, and came in the house for a while. We had a nice chat." A roar of laughter. Is that how you get all those ideas you get, from outer space?" Again chuckles of amusement.

"Go back to work," I said. Sometime the truth is more entertaining and unbelievable than a good lie. James did come out to my house in his new saucer, came in the house, and we did have a talk.

A year or so after the flying saucer landed in my yard, and I talked to James. He asked me to come for a visit. "New controls," says he, "maybe work better."

I told him when I could take some time off. "You still a Misfit on second shift?" I asked, "Haven't heard much about the old salt mine, last two or three years."

"Still Misfit," says he. "Robert still mechanic boss on second shift, Roger Burns Plant Manager now, not same now Uncle 'Soup' retired, you gone to," says he.

CHAPTER SIXTEEN
WON'T COME BACK

The old barn looked about the way it always did, there was still that hole in the roof where "anti-gravitron left and won't come back" About the only thing different was the machine. The machine that made the anti-gravitron metal was gone.

"Where's the metal machine?" I asked.

"Don't need anymore, need modulator for new controls," says he.

I wasn't about to try to unravel that mystery. Now I took his word for it, and let things be.

"James" I said, "Is this thing going to get you killed?" I asked.

"Killed?" says he, "What you mean killed?"

"James" I said, "That's a dangerous machine. You made a Wright Brother's airplane that can fly a thousand miles an hour, if not faster. High uncontrollable speed is dangerous, it can get you killed" I pleaded.

"You not 'fraid to drive race car. I learned to fly saucer, fast" said he.

A few days later I got the call I just knew I would get someday.

"Mr. Boss," sobs, "this is Margaret, James's wife," sobs, "James gone, won't come back. Maybe you can come?" she asked between sobs. As I neared the house, the barn and surrounding area looked like a war zone. Barn parts and what was now junk, was strewn about.

"Margaret" I asked, "What happened."

"James gone, won't come back. I heard a big noise, look at the barn, green smoke everywhere. When the smoke left, the barn looked like that, and the machine was gone. More sobs, James won't come back" she said.

The investigation drug out for days, people who told the truth was crack pots, and space cadets with alien encounters. And people who knew nothing about any of this, or told lies were believed.

The less, I said, the better. I said what I could say with a degree of surety, which was very little. I haven't been around James much the last few years. He said he was working on an anti-gravitron whatever that was. People talk in people questions, not one of the investigators asked machine questions. Praise the Lord!

Sometime later, Margaret called, and asked me to come out to her house. She had something she wanted to give me that belonged to James. As I came to her door, she met me with a smile that quickly became a sob.

"Come in," she said, "I got for you the stuff James said was for you to have, those twelve books too" she said, as she pointed to a stack of books.

She went through an adjacent door, and returned with a large dictionary, and a scrap book, with a picture of a flying saucer on the front.

I helped James make the scrapbook; James said I should

give this dictionary, this scrapbook and those twelve books to you. He said, I find way, you find words.

Over the next few days I leafed through the two thousand three hundred sixteen pages of the dictionary. Two hundred sixty three words had a circle around them.

The scrapbook contained accounts of flying saucers crashes, and unsubstantiated accounts of events. One that got my attention was the one near Magdalena, N.M. of the Augustine flats. Scraps of metal were supposedly found containing the manmade material #315.

The twelve books were a collection of tech manuals, with circles around certain pictures, phrases, and words.

Tree stump time, will it ever come to me?

The periodic table in one of the books, had circles around seventeen elements, plus 315, the manmade element.

PART TWO
Secrets

CHAPTER SEVENTEEN
WON'T COME BACK

I t was the spring of 1984 when I got the call, I knew, I would eventually get from Margaret. "James is gone, won't come back." Something had gone wrong with James's saucer. "Controls won't work." Was the explanation I had gotten the two times before, James was gone! So was his machine, and it was somewhat obvious what had happened by looking at the barn.

The devastation suggested an explosion according to the authorities' who investigated James' disappearance. But there was just no evidence of just what had exploded. Explosions are caused by heat, but there were no charred surfaces. It was obvious that the force of explosion came from inside the barn.

The investigation drug on for months. Everyone, including me was investigated. Those of us with firsthand knowledge were dismissed as some kind of nuts. The idea that a 'halfwit kook' like James, had somehow built a flying saucer was just too much to accept, by normal people. "Not possible!" "Where's the evidence?" Uh Hu!

James' dictionary, with the two hundred sixty-three words with circles around them, the twelve books, and James scrapbook was examined. All was dismissed as irrelevant. It was common knowledge from all accounts that James couldn't talk coherently. In short, he just babbled. By the multitude of investigators, more than one person suggested that if anyone knew what went through James' head, it was his old boss at the factory. But even that was dismissed. James worked at the factory, but James' old boss had left the factory four years ago. He was now a home builder in the community. How a carpenter could relate to flying saucers, was an enigma to say the least.

Officially James' disappearance was an ongoing investigation. It became a 'cold case' and was just no longer news worthy.

When Margaret called a couple of years later, and said she had some of James' stuff for me, I wondered what it was. James was my friend. Maybe his only good friend, at least, I was the one he confided in. Margaret and I were the only ones that really knew James, but I always had a question about how much I understood about James. Margaret had said the same thing at times.

"Mama, its misser boss!" Mattie said.

I hadn't been out to James' place for a year or so. Margaret and the kids were still living out there in the bushes. Robert Green was now the man in her life. "Mama and daddy come get the kids sometimes. Mattie wants to go, but David wants to stay home and read. He just wants to read and tear something up. He's always trying to make something. Most of the time I don't know what he' doing, maybe you know?" Margaret said. "He's out there in what's left of the barn."

"Chips off the old block," I said, "I'll go see what he's up to."

"He's making saucer, like daddy," Mattie piped up. "Maybe he won't come back. Brother like daddy, don't want girls around, they get in the way, David says!"

"Mattie, don't you like machines?" I asked.

"No, I like girl things and school," Mattie said – "Well, maybe some machines like, like computers, they're fun. David got in trouble the other day, he took one of the schools computers apart, but he put it back together. The teacher said he'd better not do it again!"

'Uh Hu," I said, "Margaret, sounds like you got your hands full. I'll go see what David's up to."

When I got to the barn, David was sitting at a table covered up with 'stuff' the boy had collected from James' machines.

"What you up to?" I asked David.

"Want to make a saucer like daddy, but don't know how. Maybe he can come back some day in his saucer," David said.

"I don't know about that," I said "we really don't know where James went, or what happened."

"You know," David said, "Daddy said you know lots of words, you can explain everything, even saucer. Mr. Boss, you know how to make saucer?" the boy asked.

"No, son," I said, "Your daddy discovered something no one on the face of the earth knows. James was my good friend, but he couldn't tell me what he knew, he said he'd find a way. I don't know how he made that saucer, nor do I know how he controlled it. But I know that something went wrong, that's why James' hasn't come back."

"David," I said, "Your mama and your grandpa tell me you read a lot. What do you read about?"

"Saucer stuff and space travel stuff, maybe I can find where my daddy went. At least I hope so!" David said.

"Uh Hu," I said, "Son a lot of science fiction is the figment of someone's imagination. They're kind of fairy tales, like the Easter bunny, and Santa Claus, and flying reindeer. But your daddy isn't a fairy tale. He actually built a flying saucer. Not too many people can believe it. Flying saucers and UFO's, to most people, are just stories. The reason people don't believe in flying saucers is because usually there's no proof. That's why people don't believe in James' flying saucer. They just can't understand such things."

"Someday, someone will discover what your daddy discovered, and will show proof, until then most people won't believe in flying saucers. The difference in your daddy and most folks was his ability to deal with the unknown in a real world. He dared to ask questions, and then find the answers. Most folks ask questions, they know the answer too, before they ask the question. Your daddy, James, was a man who dared to ask questions and then find the real answer. Son, your daddy asked questions, then found the answers other men just read about."

"Son, what are you trying to build?" I asked.

"Don't know, maybe gravitron motor that ran on gravity. Daddy made gravitron, maybe I make one," David said.

"Do you know how gravity works?" I asked the boy.

"I'll read daddy's books, maybe they will tell me," David said.

"Maybe," I said, "I need to go talk to your mama."

As I returned from my talk with David, Mattie was at the door waiting on me.

"Young lady," I asked, "how are you and school getting along?"

"Mostly I like school," Mattie said, "But sometimes the kids are mean to me and David. 'Cause of daddy's saucer. They say daddy left us because he didn't like us anymore. Is that so?"

"No Mattie, that's not so. James left because something went wrong with his machine. Not because he didn't' love his family. Mattie, your daddy was someone special. He was able to do something no other man was able to do. His work was honest and honorable, but something went wrong with his machine. Maybe in time, we will know what went wrong."

"Mattie, go play, I need to talk to Mr. Boss," Margaret said.

"Margaret, I know this is hard for you and the children. Is there anything I can do to help? That's what friends are for," I said.

"We're doing OK I guess. Momma and Daddy have been here for us. But it's the loss of James that's hard to deal with. His life was wrapped up in that machine. It possessed him. He knew there was a danger, but still he couldn't let it alone. I just don't understand such things," Margaret said as she began to sob. "I just don't understand."

"Margaret, I'm not sure I can explain what made James so special, but I do understand it. There is that something inside some men that drives them to the unknown. They just have to know what's on the other side. James somehow came to understand something no man knew before. He just had to know the outcome. James was one of the most honest men I ever knew. His endeavors were honest. His understanding was honest. And his pursuit of knowledge was honest. His ability to deal with the unknown was honest. And the final outcome was honest.

"James and his machine may be stranded on a desert isle, some place or somewhere on the other side of the universe, but he made an honest attempt to conquer the unknown. No man could let that be, at least a man like James. He couldn't let that be. It is because of the James' in this world that mankind has dared to explore the unknown. What the James' in this world have dared to discover, the rest of humanity just reads about."

"Maybe so," said Margaret, "but I just don't understand. What I do understand is that James is gone and won't come back. Now me and his children will have to get by without him. At times I almost hate him!" she began to cry.

When Margaret had regained her composure she began to tell me what James had told her to tell me. "James said you were Mis Fit like him. You know lots of stuff, and can say words. Some people just don't understand, but you did. James said that you were a man that understood gravitron saucers. You could say words. He said with his dictionary, scrapbook, those twelve books you could say words. As you know James couldn't write, but he could read. Nor could he say what he wanted too, but he could understand things. James said he wanted to be like you, a man that could say words and understand stuff. The authorities have seen James' books and dictionary, but say it makes no sense. Maybe you can understand what James was trying to say. Anyway, James said to give them to you if something went wrong. I think he knew what might happen, but did it anyway. I just don't understand," she said as the tears came again.

CHAPTER EIGHTEEN
THE BOOKS

When I got home I began to take a close look at the books and dictionary James had wanted me to have. This was obviously very important to James, those words James uttered "you say words, I find way." The secret was in these books and dictionary, but what was James trying to say? It was time for some serious tree stump sitting. Maybe the answer would come to me.

I did have one advantage. I had been James' co-worker for several years. Nobody was James boss he didn't need one, just someone to point out the problem then get out of his way. It was never that James couldn't solve a problem, more often it was his seeing the problem. When the problem was identified, James would find a solution. Sometimes his solutions defied common sense as normal people see things. I was astounded many times at the solution James would come up with. The fact was his solutions worked. It may not have been the best solution, but it was a workable solution. My problem now was, I had to learn to think like James, just find a solution to an identified problem.

It became clear to me several years ago, that James was not like most folks. Most folks can see problems not solutions. James could see solutions but not problems. What was obvious early on was how to explain the problem to James. The question to me now was, when did a saucer become a problem to James?

Now several years later, I recall an incident that may have been when the question arose, that James needed to solve.

Sometimes, men who work together, discuss things they know nothing about as if they did. Flying saucers was one of those things.

There had been a sighting recently in the neighborhood that had made the local news. We were down in the factory electric shop in one of our rare idle moments, when the discussion of the UFO came up.

"Somebody needs to figure them things out. Nobody knows for sure if they are real," somebody said.

"They real if folks can see `um," James piped up. "Maybe I think on them some."

Not long after that bull session, I heard gravitron for the first time. The simplicity of James explanation that saucers were anti-gravity motors was a plausible explanation. At the time, James thought so; could it just be that simple?

<> <> <> <> <>

"It's me again Margaret, I was looking through James' scrapbook, by chance did you help him make it?" I asked.

"Yes," she said "I helped him put all those pictures in that book. He showed me how he wanted t put in. Some are upside down, some this way and some that way. James said you would know why. I sure don't."

"Uh Hu, those words circled in the dictionary, was that done at the same time?" I asked.

"Yes, but sometimes he would put a line through the number at the bottom of the page. Sometimes he would have me put a different number on a page. I never knew what it meant. I just did what he wanted," she said.

"One more thing, those manuals, those twelve books do you know where he got them?" I asked.

"No," she said. "He had those when we got married. I never thought much about them. He'd read them kinda regular. Sometimes he would look at one, then another, maybe for hours, and then he'd go to the barn. Sometimes I'd hear a racket, sometimes I wouldn't. When that first thing went through the roof of the barn, he came to the house just laughing. It scared me and the kids to death to see him laugh," Margaret said.

He said "Little gravitron works, make a bigger one with controls, next time."

"Uh Hu, did he study the books anymore, after the thing went through the roof?" I asked.

"Mr. Boss," Margaret said "Do you know what happened to James?"

"Not yet, maybe in time, James is trying to tell me," I said.

"Nobody ask me questions like you do, James said you would understand. Like driving race car, find truth, boss find words," Margaret began to sob.

"Margaret, I know this is upsetting to you, I'm sorry, but I have to ask these questions," I apologized.

"Since I left the factory, I hadn't talked to James much. When he brought his saucer out to my house, we had a long talk, but I don't know how much I understood, about his machine. He solved more than one problem somehow, but I believe the control problem wasn't in his total control. He gave me some indication to the control problem, if I understood at all. There are large gaps in my understanding, I am trying to understand," I said.

Since I had left the factory, my house building business

had prospered. I had more work than I could do, I had to schedule my work load, where me and the men who worked for me had some time off. I was getting older. Retirement was something to think about. David McFeen was now one of my collage kids. It had been a struggle to keep him in school. Margaret had asked me to talk to him, he wanted to drop out of school, "it is boring, I can be like daddy, learn from books."

"James defied the odds," I said. "He learned to read books, but he could not write, nor could he speak plainly. He had no other choice, but you do." With the bribe of a job, he remained in school. Now he was a college student. High school had been a breeze for David, but college was a different story. Now he had to do homework, and tests now were not a snap.

James had been gone ten years now. Occasionally James' disappearance would surface in the papers, usually when an unexplained event would occur, like an occasional UFO. David, Mattie, and Margaret never had much to say about it. Over the years, Jack, Soup, and Robert Green had talked to me about James' disappearance. They were like me, space cadets. There was just no evidence, it just never happened!

But those of us who knew James, knew it did happen, and knew how. We all took the attitude 'the less said the better'. James' kids were especially troubled. The truth was too much to believe. Rumors would surface from time to time. James came from Mars and went back. He abandoned his wife and children, or was in a nut house somewhere. But, he defiantly did not build a flying saucer. There was just no proof! All of this was especially hard on James' wife and children.

Robert Green, Margaret's daddy, was now retired from the factory. He would look me up from time to time. "Are you any closer to unraveling James' mystery?" he would ask.

"Maybe," was all I could say, "Maybe someday." "Did James talk to you much, after I left the factory, about his saucer?" I asked.

"I didn't understand a word he said, about gravitron, something about control frequency. He spent a lot of time looking at Herd's Computer Theory Books and the books on Hysteresis drives. Beyond that he just did his job. When Robert Burns became plant manager, James was able to do his work. He seemed to be somewhat satisfied, but "Boss was gone, not same," is how he put it. "Boss know stuff." We all missed "Boss", Robert said.

"The Misfits were a good team, but all good things come to an end" I said. "Some of us just had to move on. I've had to move several times."

Robert and I talked about old times out at the factory, about the old Misfits, and about James. Robert said, "How's David working out for you? Margaret said you bribed him with a job, to keep him in school."

"He's a whole lot like his daddy, just tell him what you want done and leave him alone. But he's not as patient as James. He'll get frustrated when things don't go right, James just kept after it. Of course, James was twenty-two, when I got him. David's about nineteen. But he's a natural with complicated concepts, like solar energy. He is really good with his hands. He'd make a great race car driver," I said, smiling.

"As good as you were?" Robert asked.

"Probably a lot better, maybe he'd have better sense than I did," I said smiling. "You can get your neck broke, driving race cars! I don't regret those years, but I don't think I would do it again."

From time to time, I would take a look at the books and dictionary, James had wanted me to have. After tree stumpin' awhile, it finally began to sink in, what he was trying to say. Those two hundred sixty three words were the key. James must have read every last word in that huge dictionary. It wasn't the word circled, it was the definition. A word that had more than one definition, was the word circled. The number on the page was the definition to be considered. A line drawn through a page number, was an indication which definition to use.

When I compiled a list, of those two hundred sixty three words and the meanings used, it became clear what he was trying to say.

When James first came to my shift at the factory, it became clear early on, that James had an intense curiosity. He wanted to know everything about everything. Hysteresis drives was one of those things. The relation, between frequency and speed control of an AC motor, was captivating to James. The best way I could explain it to James, was by drawing circles around key words of phrases in tech manuals. Functions I would prioritize by numbers. Number one, first action, two, second action, three, etc... until the concept was concluded. That was exactly what James was now telling me! We discussed magnetism. We discussed electrical theory, computer theory, and several other subjects. It became clear to me, the student James, soon knew more than his 'Boss'. In short order, I was taking lessons, not giving them. One of the most satisfying experiences a teacher can have, is when the student excels. You've done your job!

James had given me, his friend, the inside track on a race to gravitron. But there were still answers to be found, puzzle pieces were still missing, the picture was not complete.

After I had left the factory and started my own business, my energies were now directed toward building a better house. When I was a young man in the Far East, my energies were in staying alive. As a race car driver, it was building a better car, and learning to drive it better. As a factory worker, whatever factory it was, be the best I could be. Now my major concern, was build a better house at a better price. That formula had paid real dividends for me and my business. My Grandpa was right. He used to tell me, that a man that would do a day's work for a day's pay would get more work than he could do. But new ways are always a hard sell, especially if it's new. New concepts are not convenient. Most folks want to take the easy way out, something for nothing. James knew, as I did, that real success comes from hard work. Being true to yourself is hard to do sometimes.

I knew first hand, that there was a lot of work to be done on James' saucer, especially the controls. It was the controls of James' machine that got James in trouble. The control aspect of James' invention was a tough nut to crack. I hadn't discovered that secret yet, but I had a good idea what went wrong. If I was to retrace James' steps, I had to be cautious. "Won't come back, might be a bridge of no return."

James definition:
Gravitron – a motor that runs on gravity.
Anti-gravitron – a devise that is repelled by gravity.
Control – a devise to control the repulsion of gravitron and anti-gravitron devise.

The concept was simple enough; but making concept into reality was a horse of a different color. I had to start somewhere. I tried as best I could to remember all the lessons I had taught James, about motor theory, electricity, frequency control and mechanics. What was obvious to me was how James took his first step on a thousand mile journey, in a flying saucer, that didn't come back. Without control of a devise repelled by gravity, the devise would try to escape the pull of gravity, until gravity was non-existent. The big question: Where in the universe is gravity not present?

A devise that is repelled by gravity, is mind boggling. The potential for such a devise staggers the imagination. The control of an anti-gravity devise would make space travel a reality!

One of the paradoxes I dealt with, with James, was that a problem needed an answer. James couldn't see a problem; the problem had to be explained to him. Once that was done, James could find a solution. Problems encountered along the way were speed bumps in the way. The problem was the problem. The final solution is the answer, everything else is technicalities. At least that was my understanding of James over the seven to eight years I worked with him as his boss. 'Boss' to James, was a friend who knew stuff, and could say words. Maybe even someone, who didn't understand what James, was doing.

The first devise went through the roof. The second destroyed more barn and burned James' face and hands. The third machine, blew the barn apart, and sent the machine and James to the unknown. When I asked James what happened on the way to the hospital, when the second devise blew up, I began to get an idea of what James had discovered. I got a good look at the gravitron metal machine, and I began to have some understanding, of how and why it worked. If I understood gravitron metal and gravity as James had tried to explain it to me, the control devise was some sort of frequency modulator.

James had left me a blueprint to the gravity machine, with his words in the dictionary. James was translating James language into the English language as best he could. But James' crucial things, sometimes got lost in my translation. I had seen James' gravity metal making machine, and I knew how it worked, that wasn't all that complicated. But the relation between the catalysts, that liquid in the machine, and the activating frequency was lost in translation. No explanation in the English language could explain that relation.

What I did not know about the gravitron metal machine was the strength of the magnetic field, not the frequency that activated the catalyst. A lot of educated guess work was going to be needed.

When James made his first anti-gravitron devise, he had set it off in his barn, it had gone through the roof. I didn't intend to make that mistake in my workshop. James had worked on his machine for about six years, a lot of book reading and experimenting had taken place in that six years. James left me twelve books to read. Those books were mostly dissertations on magnetism, frequency generation and control devises, for all kinds of machines. As I read and reread through James' books, I began to understand the gravitron, and what was going to be necessary to control it.

As I began to understand James' gravitron, I was becoming more certain that the control problem was what sent James out of this world. I began to build a machine out in my 'playhouse', at home in my spare time. I was able to identify the components and formula for the catalyst, that pink liquid, activated by a frequency generated by the welder's modulator. The process could turn aluminum foil into gravitron metal. The control of the process was a magnetic field, generated by electro magnets.

Once the gravitron metal was stabilized, it had the universal properties of substance called 315. When the proper frequency was resonated with 315, it became anti-gravity. It now had the exact property of gravity without controls. Gravitron metal, when excited, repulsed gravity, as sure as two magnets repel one another, with like polarity. Gravitron metal and gravity have the same polarity when excited.

A frequency shift in the gravitrons oscillation was the means of control. What James had discovered was something that works. The math, the physics, and the explanation would have to wait. The problem now was to make a flying saucer.

James was like the first man on earth that discovered fire; others would have to learn to control it! A devise that exhibited the reverse properties of gravity, boggles one's mind. The control of that devise, stagger's one's imagination. I had built devises and machines all in my adult life. Not once had the idea of a devise that defied gravity, been in my consideration until now!

James had built his saucer and had some degree of control over it. He was able to fly the thing. As crude as the saucer I saw was, it worked. When I had cautioned James about flying his machine fast, his reply was "I learned to fly fast". James had as best he could, explained the limitations of the saucer. I soon understood the strength of the anti-gravity properties of James' saucer, was directly related to the strength of the gravity. Gravity strength was not the same in all localities.

An allegory of gravitational fields is like a jet liner flying at a constant speed at thirty-five thousand feet. To maintain a constant speed, the wind direction and speed had a direct relation to fuel consumption. If fuel consumption remains constant, speed varies. Wind velocity and direction are determining factors as well. The exact relation between gravity and anti-gravity, varies with speed direction, and distance from gravity source. James was aware of the complexities of gravity. Somehow in some language, James had unraveled the complexities, and had made a machine that could operate in those 'parameters'. One of James' new words, circled in James' dictionary.

Over a long life of dealing with complex machines, I was not prepared to deal with the complexity of gravity. What went up came back down. But with anti-gravity, what went up, didn't come back down, it just kept going up! For the lack of better words, gravity and anti-gravity, have the same polarity. They repulse one another.

The gravitron material, aluminum foil converted to substance 315, needed only to be excited to have gravity properties. Gravity itself was the energy source. Anti-gravity just went along for the ride. That energizing of gravitron material was frequency saturation. Once saturated, it was anti-gravity. Without control, gravitron material would be repulsed by gravity, whatever that source of gravity was. The 'trick' James had devised for control, was altering the frequency of the gravity metal. Direction was achieved in James' saucer by disrupting the gravity wave length on part of the gravitrons base.

When I first saw James demonstrate his saucer, I noticed the 'soda cans' around the base of James saucer, those 'soda cans' were frequency generators that disrupted gravities. A power loss to that 'soda can' frequency generator would be a catastrophic. "Gravitron won't come back." I now knew as James did how to control the gravitron, unless control's failed!

When David first went to work for me, he was still in high school. My bribe had paid dividends. David would soon be graduating from college, with a degree in computer. When I dealt with computers back in the early sixties, they couldn't compare to the technology of today. Each time I moved on in my life, it wasn't that I lost interest; it was something more interesting came along. Usually it was a new machine with a new technology that got my interest. I had moved from radio and T.V. to computers, from computers to airplanes, and from airplanes to racecars, then to race car construction and driving. My mother's death put me in a holding pattern, and I became a factory worker. That factory work brought me into contact with James.

James and I became a two way street. He wanted to know what I knew, and now I wanted to know what he knew. James knew or learned, as I did, that you just can't explain some things to some people. Some things can only be explained to some people in different languages. Explaining something to your wife and children can be done in words, sometimes. It comes by love and admiration for someone you care deeply for. It's like sitting by your wife in a moment of crisis, nothing can be said, you just know.

Language, any language, is inaccurate at times. Sometimes, you just know, but stumble in trying to explain. The pain I saw in David's eyes, made me reluctant to talk about James. David seemed to want to forget the day James disappeared. The truth about James' saucer was as unbearable to James wife and children, as it was to me. Unbelief is a bitter pill to swallow. James knew things no human on earth knew, and in honesty had acted on that knowledge. The final outcome was unbelievable.

I had seen, I had believed, but I didn't understand. No one else had seen, no one else could believe, and who could understand what they had not seen or believed. James had left me the blueprints to the unbelievable and the un-understandable. I had talked to Margaret from time to time, and I had told her what I knew. I now had James' secret. I knew what went wrong. I had that secret; it had taken nearly fifteen years. There was a real danger in what I now knew. Who should I tell the secret to? Margaret said in time she would tell her children. I knew what had happened to James, and I had told Margaret.

My children had been gone from home for several years. They were all out making their marks in the world. I had several grandchildren, and the promise of great-grandchildren. My wife had been diagnosed with a serious respiratory illness some time ago, and I was in the process of liquidating my business. I would soon be retiring. My heart just wasn't into working all the time. I guess I was getting old and tired. However I was still in good physical health that is for an old man!

David, now out of college, was off on his own. He had a good job that paid well. I had gotten a graduation notice from Mattie. She was due to graduate soon from my Alma Mater. All of the McFeen family called me Mr. Boss. Mattie especially liked to call me 'Misser Boss' I guess it was a kid thing. I had always taken special delight in tormenting her as she grew up. Now she was a pretty young woman about to graduate from college.

Because of James and our relationship, I took more than casual interest in James' children. In many respects, David and Mattie were like my own grandchildren, and I saw them about as often.

I sat with Margaret and David at Mattie's graduation ceremonies. I had been with Margaret and Mattie at David's graduation last year. After the ceremony, I asked Margaret, "Do you want me to talk to your children yet?"

"Not yet, maybe next year," Margaret said.

Mattie and David went to receive their earned congratulations from friends and relatives. Margaret and I were left alone for the moment.

"Mr. Boss," Margaret said, "would you and your wife, if she's able, come out to my house tomorrow evening? I want you to talk to my children while David is still here. Mattie will want to leave with him, I'm sure, to job hunt. You know how kids are."

"I'll be there, don't know if she can make it, what time?" I said.

It had been awhile since I had been to James' place. It was still at the end of a cow trail. Margaret had maintained her home, for her and the children. Outside of a few close relatives and me, James' place was unknown and unseen by the public. Over the last fifteen years, few remembered James' disappearance.

James had been gone, nearly fifteen years. At the time I had a fair idea of what went wrong. After receiving James' dictionary, scrapbook and the twelve tech manuals, and after doing lots of study, I knew exactly what went wrong.

After more study and experimenting, I was able to make a gravitron machine that made gravitron metal. The next problem was to find the circumstance that turned gravitron metal into an anti-gravitron devise. That took a while. When I had given James lessons in Helix Arc welding, he was more concerned with the frequency metals would fuse together, than the welding technique. Any welder can tell you metals react differently at different amperages and frequency. The covering agent, or flux, also changes the reaction. It was a matter of finding the frequency and cover agent that 'excited' gravitron metal.

A picture of a Helix Arc machine in James' scrapbook was upside down. On the same page, was a picture of the same machine, sideways. When I saw James' demonstration of his saucer, I noticed James' Helix Arc machine was lying on its side. I now wished I had asked why. In time I discovered why.

Margaret and James' children seem to be waiting my arrival. Margaret's mother and daddy were there as well. Robert Green and I had been co-workers and good friends for many years. We had been Misfits He had asked me several times since James had disappeared if I was any nearer to unraveling the James mystery.

As guest of honor at a fine meal, maybe it was time for me to explain my appearance, by Margaret's request.

"I don't know where to start," I said "just take off at a dead run, I guess. Margaret and I have talked a lot about James' disappearance, over the last couple of years. Margaret decided, with my agreement, to wait until Mattie was out of school to talk to you two children about James disappearance. Your grandfather and grandmother have every right to know what I know as well. I know what happened to James. I believe I know exactly what went wrong.

"I have had James' secret in my sole possession for about two years. Your mother wanted the secret kept until Mattie graduated. Margaret was afraid; as I was that you children would quit school and go after James, when you knew what I now know. I am now prepared to divulge James secret to you children."

With stunned expressions, the children was speechless.

"This is going to take a while, a very long while. It took James about ten years of hard work to build his saucer. Unraveling the mysteries, took most of that time. It has taken me the better part of fifteen years to retrace James' steps, and he left me a blueprint! Your mother and I will tell you all the details, of the secret James left behind in those twelve books, his scrapbook, and the dictionary your mother gave to me about two years after James disappeared. James wanted me to have them, so I could "say the words." Before any of this will make an ounce of sense to you children, you'll have to learn a new language. That language only James knew, and he taught it to me. If you children are willing to work hard, I'll teach that James language to you. You people, James' family, have a lot to talk over."

"Robert," I said, "we've worked together in the past, you, have a pretty good idea of what I am saying. Margaret and I want you to talk to your grandchildren, tell them what's at stake, both the good and the bad."

For James' children, this was a shocker. They had rather well dealt with James' disappearance, as something like a bad dream, somewhere in the distant past. Now, the nightmare was back. Now those two children would have to deal with this again, in real time. In their past, when they awoke, the nightmare would fade. Now when they awoke, the nightmare remained.

"Mr. Boss, this is Margaret, me and my family had a long talk about what you said the other night. Daddy told the kids to not go off half-cocked. That what you know is too important to make snap decisions. David went back to his job and girlfriend. Mattie said she was going to take a vacation from studies for a while. I'm not sure they want to know all the details about

James. They were so young when he left. I guess we'll wait a while and see what they decide to do. Daddy said he would come and talk to you in a few days."

CHAPTER NINETEEN
BELIEVED

"Old friend," I said, "How's the world treating you these days? How's retirement?"

"My retirement is just like yours, I need a job so I can rest," Robert said. "People can find more things for you to do, than you can do. And everybody knows if you're retired, you got time on your hands, and you don't need to be paid." Robert complained.

"That's the way I see it," I said, "but now my wife can't run interference for me. Now I got kids and grandkids wanting me to slow down – right after I get through with their project. I'm thinking I need to hustle up me a new job so I can get some rest."

"Well, at least I still have a wife. She's old and cranky, but she still looks out for me," Robert said. "I came to talk to you about James' saucer. Margaret told me and her mother awhile back, that you figured out what James had done. She also said why she wanted the secret kept."

"Now that the kids know, that you know, what happened to their daddy. What have you decided to do about it? The whole world wants to know what you know. I can't imagine, what that is like," Robert said.

"I got to tell you the God's honest truth, there are times

I wish I didn't know James' secret. And I'm not sure I want those kids to know. I've thought more than once, that the secret should die with me, and it will, unless I tell someone!" I said to Robert. "Let's go out to my playhouse, I want to show you my latest toy."

"Well," Robert said "this kinda looks like James barn, before it blew up. I take it you and gravitrons have an understanding."

"How much of James work, out in his barn did you see?" I asked.

"Not much, first off, I didn't have a clue what he was doing. He couldn't tell me. Everybody knew you and James lived in a different world. Some of us even dared to wonder, if both of you were from another planet. Some folks thought James just went back to where he came from. I guess you've heard all that?" Robert said.

"I've heard all that a few times. One of those investigators made that suggestion. He said I needed to go after James, and when I found him stay there. He said the world didn't need any more space aliens. Did James show you 'gravitron metal'?" I asked.

"No," Robert said, "I heard him mention a new metal."

"Here's a piece," I said as I picked up the piece of shiny metal, on my work table. "See if you can bend it."

"It looks like a thin sheet of aluminum. My God! What is this stuff?" Robert exclaimed.

"That's gravitron metal. That was the first secret James unraveled. That once was a piece of aluminum foil that was converted to substance 315. Let me show you how it's done," I said.

I took the box of aluminum foil, pulled out a few inches; I placed it inside my machine that looked like a microwave oven.

When I turned it on, the piece of aluminum foil rose to the center of the machine. That faint green glow was evident. The machine quit making its hum, the metal settled back down, I opened the door and handed Robert the piece of metal.

"Gravitron metal," I said, "Now do you want to see what happened to James' barn? Let's go outside." I gathered up a piece of equipment, a 'black box' and the gravitron metal. I set the box down, placed the gravitron metal on top, I turned the device on and handed Robert a pair of glasses. It'll take a minute or so. Soon the metal vanished, but a faint green trail leading to the heavens remained. "Gravitron left won't come back, no controls," I said in James language. "That green glow you've seen is Zeta particle radiation. That's what caused those burns James got. Fortunately he had on his glasses. Zeta can be fatal, without protection. Blue tinted glass is about all you need, but you can still get bad sunburned, if you're close to the Zeta source. Zeta enters the brain through the retina of the eye."

"I take it there is much more to this than what I've just seen," Robert said.

"Much more. Much, much more. What you've just seen could put a man in space, if controllable. The real problem, is putting the genie back in the bottle, it's as simple as that," I said.

"I've seen enough," Robert said, more than enough. "I can hardly believe what I have just seen, and I sure don't understand what I've just seen."

"Welcome to James' world," I said, smiling.

"I'm going to do just what I used to do, back when we were misfits. I'm going home. When you get it figured out, tell me what I can do to help. I don't have to understand any of this. Such stuff makes my head hurt," Robert said, smiling.

'Misser Boss' this is Mattie, "Mama says I need to talk to you. I had a long visit with grandpa, he was telling me about your demonstration. Well I talked to David and he said the next time he was down, he'd like to see your trick, if you can do it again."

"Mattie, that wasn't a trick and I can do it again," I said.

"I guess that was the wrong word to use. I'd like to see how that was done too.

Grandpa said, he just couldn't believe what you showed him. Grandpa said, you really do know what happened to my daddy. Do you really know?" Mattie asked.

"Yes, Mattie, unfortunately I really know what happened – and why."

CHAPTER TWENTY
DEMONSTRATION

It was about two months before Mattie called again. "Mister Boss', David came down yesterday. He said he'd like to see you're demonstration. So would I, when would be a good time?"

"Just about any time that is convenient for you. I'm home a lot, now That I'm retired. I'm always here, unless I'm gone," I said.

"About noon tomorrow, we'll bring a pizza." Mattie said.

"Pizza, you say, maybe I can make some tea. If I can remember how," I said.

"David" I said, "I thought maybe you'd forgot me, since you became a cyborg with a good job."

"Not hardly," David said, "I don't think I ever thanked you for giving me that job that kept me in school."

"No thanks necessary, good hands are hard to come by these days. You're a lot like your daddy was, you'll do well," I said. "Let's go out to my playhouse. It's where I keep all the new stuff. James left me the blueprints."

"First things first," I said, "How much do you children know about James' work?"

"Really, not much," David said. "Mama didn't like talking about it much. All she ever told us, was 'Mr. Boss' could explain it, if anyone could. But it was so upsetting to mama, we just let things be. She did say that daddy wanted you to have a bunch of old books and his dictionary. Why anyone would give someone a dictionary is beyond me."

"I remember daddy's dictionary," Mattie said. "It was a great big one. He used to read it a lot."

"That dictionary and those books is how I was able to 'say the words' James found a way to tell me his secret. He couldn't write or talk plainly, but he found a way to tell me what he knew. I had a real advantage. James worked for me several years. I had a very close relationship with him. As a boss, you'd better know the people who work for you, better than they know themselves. In a factory with lots of machinery, you can get people hurt, if you don't know who's having a bad day when they come to work."

"I knew within a week that James was not going to be like anyone I had ever run across. James scared people. People fear most what they don't understand. James was a hard study, even for me, but I understood his problem. I had seen it before. I had been rejected as a kid for exactly the same reasons. What made a difference in my life was being adopted at twelve years of age. A new environment and a really good teacher, made a difference. With a good education, people expected you to know 'stuff'. Lots of 'stuff', maybe even useful 'stuff.' Real experience, in the real world, comes with a demonstration of your worth. You have to learn, to put up or shut up."

"James had what appeared to be a handicap. He couldn't talk plainly or write. That handicap was probably his greatest advantage. Look at Steven Hawkins with all his handicaps. James knew at an early age, he was not like everybody else. To succeed he'd have to try harder than most folks. His efforts paid off. Like a lot of folks with handicaps, he became exceptional. Anyone around James any length of time knew his problem solving ability was extraordinary."

"This saucer thing, for James, was just a problem that needed a solution. It was just that simple. Somehow, he decided to solve gravity. It was simple to James. Flying saucers ran on gravity, like motors that run on electricity. Like poles, repel one another, unlike poles attract. Electricity, magnetism, and gravity, were all similar, but were different. Isolate gravity, and make it work for you. That's how electricity and magnetism became useful tools, why not gravity?"

"Enough of this talk for now. Let's go see what you think of gravitron metal. You came for a demonstration, not a lecture," I said.

When we came into my playhouse, David said, "Wow, look at this stuff, it looks a lot like daddy's barn used to."

"I remember seeing things like this when I was a little kid," Mattie said.

"It should look familiar, James left the blueprints. I just followed his yellow brick road," I said. "Let's start with this," I handed a piece of metal to David. "What do you make of it?" I asked.

"It looks like a piece of aluminum, what's special about it?" David asked, while Mattie looked on.

"See how it bends." David casually began to apply pressure, to the unyielding metal. Then more pressure.

"There's a vise and hammer, give them a try," I said, smiling.

David put the metal in the vise, and hit it with the hammer. But it made no noise, nor did it bend. "I certainly have never seen or heard of anything like this stuff. Not even in physics or chemistry," David said.

Mattie asked, "What is this stuff?"

"According to computer modeling, it exhibited the qualities of substance 315." I said.

"I've never seen or heard of a substance 315, on any periodic chart, everything above 235 is manmade and unstable. How did you come by this stuff?" David asked.

"Oh, I made it, you want ta' see how?" I said.

"I got to see this," said a skeptical David.

"See that box of aluminum foil? Pull out about six to eight inches. Put it in my microwave oven. Turn the oven on. Stand back and watch the show. It'll take about a minute."

David turned on the machine; the piece of aluminum levitated in the machine, and started to radiate that green glow. When the machine quit its hum, the metal settled back down.

"You've just made your first piece of gravitron metal. Take it out of the oven, it's not hot. See what you think of it," I said, smiling.

David retrieved the metal. After some examination, he handed it to Mattie. "They don't teach this stuff in college, at least not where I went," David said.

"How'd you do that?" Mattie said.

"I followed James' blueprints," I said, smiling.

"No. I mean how'd the machine do it?" David asked.

"I'd have to do some fancy guesswork to explain, a molecular shift. But there's a lot more to this stuff. You want to see it in action?" I asked. Take these glasses with you. Let's go outside. Bring your metal with you. I'll get my black box, and eye protection, Zeta particle radiation."

"I don't think I dare ask what a Zeta particle is," Mattie said.

"I'll explain Zeta particles later. Now David, put your metal on this back box, and you children put your glasses on, to watch the show." I turned the black box on, "it'll take about a minute. Watch closely, or you'll miss the show."

The metal vanished and a light green ray of light ascended toward the sky. 'Anti-gravitron won't come back," I said.

When the demonstration ended, Mattie was all smiles. David was shaking his head. "I just don't believe this, it's just not possible... not possible," David said "not possible."

After the demonstration, we went to my house to have the pizza and tea. Mattie was all excited, but David was still in denial.

"I just don't believe what I just saw," David said, "There has to be an explanation that makes sense. I had lots of physics and chemistry in college, if what I just saw is real, I wasted a college education. You and daddy, my daddy, have been living in a world that I didn't know existed. This just can't be!" David said.

"David," Mattie said, "quit being so obtuse. You don't have to understand everything, to believe in some things. What we have just seen, is out of this world by now."

"But, they don't teach that stuff, in my college," David said.

"They didn't teach it in mine either," Mattie said angrily.

"Yoo-Hoo," I said, "They didn't teach this back in the stone age, when dinosaurs like me went either. What we went to college for was to learn to think. Don't they teach critical thinking anymore? They do in the schools of hard knocks, where James and I were students. I have a college education too. But, I can tell you the schools of hard knocks is a far better teacher."

"James figured out a flying saucer, by critical thinking. He challenged the prevailing attitudes of common knowledge, and dared to challenge the unknown. He wasn't confused by facts, other people's facts. He made up his own mind. He acted with the courage of his convictions. That is absolute honesty!"

"Well, I want to know more, a whole lot more. 'Misser Boss' and my daddy knows more than me and you put together," Mattie said.

"Misser Boss', how did daddy get from gravitron metal to a flying saucer? I remember seeing daddy saucer out in the barn, before it blew up, now I know why. The investigators couldn't figure out how the barn blew up. It didn't blow up; it was in the way when the controls failed. Isn't that what happened?" Mattie observed.

"Do you know how daddy made his saucer?" Mattie asked.

"Yes," I said, James left me his blueprints. He also left me a blue print to the control problem. That's still to be solved. The controls for James' saucer were not stable, under certain conditions. There is more work to be done. That's what James was doing, when he and his saucer vanished."

After a long pause, when Mattie finally ran down, "Mister Boss," David said, "The problem – the control problem – was it a fluctuating energy source?"

"Well now," I asked David, "how did you arrive at that conclusion, that quick?"

"Maybe my college education wasn't a total waste after all," David said. "Do you still have daddy's books?" David asked.

"They're in my library, along with my notes. Are you children planning on doing some homework?" I asked.

"Not today, I got a job and a girlfriend up in Tulsa. But, I'll be back, maybe with a wife. I haven't told mama yet, and you'd better not blab," David said to Mattie.

"You mean the blond?" Mattie piped up.

"She's a lot like mama. She has good sense. She's not like you, a know it all," David said, and then added "You're a blabber mouth. I'll tell mama, when I want mama to know."

"I see you children get along well. About like mine used too," I said, smiling. "Would you folks like to take a look at James' books? They're in my library," I said.

"Sis," David said, "You're not going to believe his library. He has lots of books, especially books on solar energy. He knows as much about solar energy as daddy did flying saucers. I've been in his library many times. I don't remember seeing daddy's books in there."

"They weren't in the library until I knew you children were going to come out. They were by my bed. They put me to sleep, many nights, over the last several years. It took me several years to figure out James' language. The dictionary was the key to translation. My notes are not with James books. My notes, will explain, gravitron, anti-gravitron, levitation and the control problem. It took me fifteen years to understand what James did. James knew what he was onto, but he couldn't say the words."

Anyone who has been on the cutting edge of anything has had trouble explaining things. There are no words for the things unknown. I had exactly the same problem as a kid. I could build things, but couldn't explain how I could do it. I still have that problem. Some things you just know, there is no language for it. Complicated subjects are hard to explain. With enough background in a subject, you can usually catch on fairly quick. I must caution you now, things get lost in translation.

This I tell you now, I have the skills to build a saucer, but I am not at this time able to control it. James also knew the 'gravity', not a pun, of his discovery. No man could walk away from that discovery. That's them on the desk. My notes are tucked away for now," I said.

"Can we look at daddy's books?" Mattie asked.

"You can have them. They rightfully belong to you children. I have my notes. I don't need these books anymore. But you will need to know what's in those books if you decide to continue James' work. We'll talk about this after you have had a chance to look at your daddy's books" I said.

'Misser Boss', can I come here and study daddy's books? If David don't mind, I'd rather they stayed here," Mattie said.

"I believe those books would be better off here, at least for now. If you'll let me, I'd like to do my homework here too," David said.

"You're welcome in James' world. Those books in time, belong in a museum somewhere. James is gone, and I'm older than dirt, if I live to be an old man, I don't have long to live. One of the investigators' that investigated James' disappearance said to me *'you need to go after James, and when you find him, stay with him. The world, don't need any more space aliens!'* That may have been good advice" I said.

CHAPTER TWENTY-ONE
STUDY TIME

Mattie became a frequent visitor to my library. She would pour over the tech manuals. "I just don't understand. About the time I think I understand, some other explanation puts me back to where I started. How could you and daddy make any sense out of this stuff?" Mattie said, frustrated.

"It takes a while," I said, "it's like Rome; it wasn't built in a day."

David would come by now and then. His greatest interest of late, was a young woman. "My job in Tulsa," David said, "has possibilities and promises a future. Daddy's saucer, promises excitement and self-destruction."

I faced those same choices as a young man. I chose the excitement, the challenges, and the risk. I drove race cars. Knowing each time I buckled-up, I could self-destruct. There were times, a great number of times, when competitors tried to help me down that road to destruction. It was a risk I was willing to take, so long as I was in control. Control meant knowing the difference between taking a chance and taking a calculated risk.

James had taken a chance, not a calculated risk. I had taken chances and wound up, upside down, or in the midst of a multi-car pileup, more than once. Staying out of trouble comes with experience. Your win and loss percentage depends on finishing the race you're in. Calculated risk, means finishing. Taking unnecessary chances usually means last place, and a mangled mess for a car.

I did not intend to take the chance James took, nor did I intend to let James' children take needless chances.

The day, I knew would come, when James' children would want to take up where James had left and didn't come back.

My playhouse was what used to be my workshop. I built parts or machinery for my solar house business. Some things like solar trackers, needs devises unnamed, or un-buyable. I just made what I needed. My shop was well equipped with the latest do-dads.

I had worked several years as a millwright and factory worker. But now that I was at home with my ailing wife, I had time on my hands to tinker – with – flying saucers.

When I was certain I had unraveled James secrets, I began to build the hardware James had left me the blueprints for. Most of the technical knowledge for James' saucer, came from books and experiments. James had left me the bread crumbs to follow. Our close relationship had given me a real advantage, not only that, but I had been the source of a lot of James' high tech technology.

He had built on what I knew and what he had gleaned out of books. Then he had gone out to his barn and put guess work to the test. Like all great discoveries, sometimes just plain dumb luck plays a roll.

Maybe the catalyst concoction was a product of dumb

luck, maybe an educated guess, or maybe trial and error. What was a fact, the combination of elements in the pink liquid, at a generated frequency within a known straight magnetic field, would produce gravitron material.

How James arrived at that formula, is unimportant. What is important was the fact it worked.

It had been about two years since I had told Margaret that I had unraveled James' secret. "Now that you know what James did, are you going to build a saucer?" Margaret asked.

"I don't know yet." I said to her. "The potential for James discovery could change the world we live in. I'm not sure the world is ready for a change like that. When your children are old enough, maybe they should decide. James wanted me to say the words, that's why he left me his notes. Now I can say the words, at least most of them, but I'm not sure I should. There is some real danger I have uncovered as well. It's like nuclear energy, once the genie is out of the bottle, you can't put it back."

"Well, David is out of school now and Mattie will finish next year. Mattie is so impulsive, if you tell her what you know, she'll quit school. It's been hard for me to keep these kids in school, as you well know. I want to see Mattie graduate," Margaret said.
"You can tell me when to talk to them," I said.

"Maybe next year," Margaret said.

"Margaret," I said, "I need to ask you a hard question. What do you think those children of yours will do about James' work?"

"They've both been hurt badly by James' disappearance. They've lived with the snide remarks, the subjections, and the downright meanness of uncaring people all their lives. David may just want to forget about it, and get on with what he sees as a normal life, but Mattie may want to get even for what people have done to her. We don't talk about James, or his disappearance. It's just too painful."

After this conversation two years ago, I began to make preparation for the saucer construction. Two things concerned me, first was my age, second, what about James' secret? His secret was in my notes now. Not in the twelve books, the dictionary, and the scrapbook. They were road maps if you knew where you were going, and could think in James language. That language, only James and I knew. We had invented it, in the years we worked together. Now, only I knew James secret.

My home was off the beaten path, there was only one way in down a tree lined path. When I ran a business, I did so from town. Now that I was retired and mostly alone, not too many visitors made their way down the road to my house, except for the few health care workers. Those who did, called first. My home was very large; I had built it when I had a family and four children at home. My children, now had children, and soon I would be a great grandfather. I had grandchildren, David and Mattie's age, and I knew that I did not have the stamina to keep up with their youth. I was going to need an early start!

James had left me in a cloud of dust! It had taken me several years to catch up. I knew James' kids had the same potential. I had busied myself with making preparations. I had built an addition to my playhouse, with a retractable roof several years ago. In that addition was the equipment necessary to build the saucer. That was not a major undertaking for a man with my skills. I had been, after all, James' teacher, in welding and mechanics.

The control problem for a saucer that was repulsed by gravity provided some real challenges. Letting the genie out of the bottle was relatively simple, putting the genie back in the bottle was going to take some doing, as I well understood. "Controls don't work. Won't come back." Was disaster in the making!

The first time I saw James' saucer, it was a 'thing', it was a metal stock trough, with a lawn chair sitting in the middle. The control, according to James, was in a box under his lawn chair. The control of that mass of metal 315, was the frequency oscillator in the box under the seat. Elevation was achieved, by the control of anti-gravity forces! Direction was achieved by the magnetic field inherent in the earths mass. That seemed simple enough, but a lot easier said than done. The real fly in the ointment was speed. At high speed, control is harder to achieve. The repulsion of gravity is exactly at one hundred eighty degrees. It remains at one hundred eighty degrees from the gravity source which is also the magnetic source. The magnetic source is at right angles to gravity. The equation changes with speed.

James' solution to all these variables was a mechanical servo system, not computers. Servos depend on variations in the available signal energy received, generated by movement. In short, the more energy received the more movement. The less energy received the less movement. Once the energy source is no longer received the controls are nonexistent, the departure is at one hundred eighty degrees to the source of gravity.

So long as there is a constant energy source, servo systems work remarkably well. James was using batteries for the control energy source.

When James disappeared, the control energy source failed from the offset. Once the anti-gravity source was engaged, the devise was on a trip to the end of gravity.

James was flying his saucer within the parameter of his understanding. His limits were: altitude, lack of oxygen, movement, G forces, and positioning, line of sight, and visibility. His saucer was capable of exceeding all of his limitations.

For the next two years, I seldom saw David. He now had a young wife to keep his mind off of saucers. A good woman kept

James grounded for a while, but eventually the call of a flying saucer returned.

Mattie at first came often to study James' book, and ask questions. But as the questions became more complex, she seemed to become more agitated and impatient. To her, sometimes my answers seemed evasive.

"Sometimes, you talk in riddles," she'd say. And I would point out "There are just no words in English to describe the relations between 'this and that', the best that I can explain the relation between speed and control comes with experience. At least that is how it works with a race car. A good race car is capable of a lot more speed than you can control. With experience, a driver learns to control the car at a higher speed. There are a great number of variables, like weight distribution, tire pressure, tire composition, track conditions, weather conditions, and how you feel. That's just a few of the variables. How well you deal with all these variations will determine whether you win, lose or wind up in a heap! All those variables change during the course of a race." I said to her.

Mattie, there are no words in my vocabulary to tell you what it's like to be in control of a race car at high speed with all the unknown you deal with. But those people, who have competed on a race track, know exactly what I am saying. It's an unwritten language, but some people understand.

Mattie, your daddy and I had a very close relationship, in the midst of machines, by day I was Boss, but in saucer, James was Boss. The common thread between James and I was a language he and I understood.

"Well, I just don't understand all this gravitron stuff," Mattie said, dejected.

"Mattie, James didn't understand all there is to know about gravitron, and saucer motors. But he was willing to learn.

He dared to challenge what he didn't know, and act upon what he did know. James never lost track of where he wanted to go. There is an old saying I heard as a child, "If you don't know where you're going, any road will get you there" I said.

"Misser Boss, can I take daddy's books home? Maybe I can spend more time learning gravitron" Mattie asked.

"Those books belong to you and David. James wanted me to say words TO-HIS_CHILDREN. James wanted his children to know, but he couldn't say the words, he hoped I could. Mattie I was probably James' best friend, except for your mother. And James became one of my best friends over the years. James and I were the only soldiers in our own personal wars. We helped each other. When James didn't come back, I knew the day would come when I would have to 'say words'. James was my friend. I had to say words, but only to his children, and maybe to myself." I said.

"Well, David don't seem to be in much of a hurry. That wife of his seems to have him on a leash. What's she got going for her?" Mattie complained.

"Mattie," I said smiling, "I sure can't explain that to you."

CHAPTER TWENTY-TWO
SAUCER

I had built my version of a kiddie swimming pool out of the gravitron metal. As long as the gravitron metal didn't become excited with the frequency of oscillation, the saucer remained earth bound. But when the frequency resonated in the metal it became anti-gravity. Or, more correctly, became the same polarity of gravity. How strong the anti-gravity forces in the saucer, were determined by the transfer of the properties of anti-gravity back to metal 315. Once excited metal 315 became anti-gravity; and that was the trick, transforming anti-gravity metal back to 315.

James had built his gravitron machine out in his barn. I had built my version in my playhouse, with a retractable roof. James had built his house out of parts from an airplane salvage, so had I.

The saucer James had landed in my yard would pass for something from outer space. My version had solar panels integrated into the surface. They were designed to recharge the battery, not a great amount of energy was required for control. But it had to be stable. Fluctuations had to be eliminated.

In the two years since I had talked to James' children, I had been busy building my own saucer version. It was nearing completion. I hoped to have a test run soon.

"Margaret," I said over the phone, "Have your kids been around lately? I haven't seen either one in some time."

You know how kids are, they are too busy to be bothered by the old folks. But they will be here this week-end" Margaret said.

"Well tell them I'd like to see them, if they have time to come by" I said.

I got a call Sunday afternoon. "Misser Boss, this is Mattie. David and I can come by for a few minutes this evening" she said.

When David and Mattie arrived, we had the usual howdy's, when they were over, I invited them out to my play-house. "I've been kind of busy of late. By the way, have you thought about James' saucer lately?" I asked.

"I've been busy with my job" David said. "I have read daddy's books. I think I understand some of the logic of gravity, and it's relation to frequency, according to dad's books and dictionary. But there are a lot of gaps in my understanding. In time I would like to experiment with the saucer technology, but not now. I've got other things to think about."

"What about you, Mattie?" I asked.

"I don't think I understand any of it. I guess, I'm stupid, but I sure like the idea." Mattie said.

"Uh hu" I said.

We entered the door to my playhouse. Would you like to see my new toy?" I asked, smiling.

I opened the door to the new addition, and turned on the lights. "What do you think?" I asked. Those two youngsters just stood there, speechless.

"WOW, look at that" at last Mattie said. "Does it work?"

"I don't know," I said, "it's not ready for a test run yet."

"Mr. Boss," David said at last, "I see you certainly have been busy. I kinda knew what you were up to, when we built this new addition to your workshop, back when I was working for you. We wondered about solar panels on the roof that opened up. But with what we saw in your solar business, it didn't have to make sense. We just figured you knew what you were doing. With what little we talked about dad while I worked for you, I kinda understood, you and dad were onto something. But then dad vanished, and nobody believed the truth. You and dad were labeled kooks, space cadets was what I heard as a kid growing up. The less said about UFO's the better for us and I guess you too."

"You're going to fly the thing, aren't you? Even knowing it might not come back." David said.

"Well, I'd fly it, if I ever got the chance." Mattie said.

"Building flying saucers makes a good retirement occupation." I said. "It keeps me active. Maybe more than I want to be."

A few days later, I got a call. "Misser Boss, when me and David told mama you had a saucer out in your workshop, she freaked out. We didn't intend to upset her, we didn't even know it would. She's just not the same anymore. She's going on about daddy being gone, and now you'll soon be gone. We told her it didn't fly, but she said it would. She said, she knew you and daddy. You just couldn't leave well enough alone. Now it's all come back," Mattie said concerned.

"Mattie, do I need to talk to her?" I asked.

"She says she don't want to talk to anybody about saucers. Besides, she says, now a flying saucer is going to kill her kids," Mattie said.

"Uh hu," was all I could say.

"I think I will quit my job and come home, maybe that will help. Besides, I don't really like my job, it's boring. Maybe I could find me a job around here."

"Uh Hu," I said.

CHAPTER TWENTY-THREE
MAIDEN FLIGHT

I t had been about a month since James' children had seen the saucer. I was making the final preparation, for its maiden flight. I must admit I was feeling a little apprehensive about this. It was kinda like buckling up in a new race car. You really don't know what to expect, until you have taken a lap or two. I had checked the controls again and again – then again! There comes that moment, Sit down, Shut up, Buckle up, and Turn it on! Then deal with the rush that is sure to come.

I had opened the roof in anticipation, now it was time. I flipped the switch, the saucer came to life. The console with all its meters, and T.V. screens, began to show data. I now held the joy stick in my hand. I gently pulled straight up. The machine began to rise. When I had cleared the roof, I moved the stick in the direction I wanted to go, ever so gently after a maiden flight. I brought the saucer back through the hole in the roof. When it was back on the earth, I gave a complete check of the instruments on the console in front of me. I breathed a sigh of relief. Maybe I had been holding my breath! It works – it works – was all I could say to myself. I believe it's gonna work! But you better go slowly, I said to myself.

I just sat there in the dark, relishing, my accomplishment. At last reality returned. What happened to the lights? Florescent – Zeta Radiation – Poof! Turn the lights off next time.

Margaret called, "Mr. Boss, can I talk to you? Since James died, I don't know anyone else except you and your wife."

"Why certainly we can talk. What are friends for?" I said.

"It's Mattie, she says she aims to quit her job and get her an apartment in town, so she can be closer to me. Misser. Boss, it's not me, it's that saucer. That's all she wants to talk about. Saucer, saucer, saucer! Saucers scare me to death! A saucer possessed James, now its possessing my children! And it possessed you years ago!" she said between sobs.

"Margaret, I don't know what to say. James wanted me to tell his children of his work. 'you say words, I find way, you say words' was the way he put it to me, as you well know."

"I know all that," Margaret said, sobbing. "But, I'm scared. I just don't know what makes this so important. It took my husband, it's taking you my only friend, and now it is taking my children. I don't know what to do. Flying saucers are *EVIL!*"

"Margaret, James came to know somehow, things that no one on earth knew. No man could let that be, without telling someone. James knew it was just to important to hide, especially from his children. At the time they were just tykes, but now their grown, with college educations. Maybe they do need to know how great their daddy was. He was the bravest and most honest man I ever knew. In spite of all that, his handicap consumed him. Some people just can't tolerate handicaps, because of their own inadequacies. That handicap may have been James' greatest advantage. Honest work gave him an identity, among the human race, his work was important. It was really important, but his wife and children were more important. He wanted his wife and children to benefit from his work. James was well aware of what he was onto. It didn't take long for me to know too. I wanted to help him, what I could. He was my friend that made it important to me. It still is, I owe it to James and his children. Thanks to James, I now know what he knew, and maybe more. What I now know, no one else knows, nor will they know in the short term, unless I tell them. I haven't told your children all I know. I may decide to die with James' secret," I said.

"Now I don't know what to say," Margaret said, "but this saucer thing scares me."

"Margaret," I said, "I believe we fear most what we understand least. This saucer thing scares me also, so did race cars at first. In time they didn't, they were a machine I controlled. Not a machine that controlled me, like they were when I first started racing."

"I just don't understand, this saucer thing scares me. You scare me. James scared me. Now, my children scare me." Margaret confessed.

The saucer was now a reality. It could fly, but how well? Where? Would it come back? The limits were not the machine. The machine was far better than the man who created it. The machine James and I had created could fly higher and faster than earth bound men could endure. The limits were not the machine, the limits were human. The parameters were flesh and blood, not gravity and magnetism. James had by accident, exceeded human limits. His machine, intact, was somewhere. And wherever that machine was, James was there also, dead. For no human body could survive without the necessities of human existence, oxygen, water, food and warmth. None of those necessities did James have.

The new machine was equipped with a controlled environment capsule, life sustaining for a short duration. I had incorporated what I knew into the new machine. Those years I had spent in the aircraft industry, was a great source of technology, as was my basic knowledge of computers, gained at White Sands, New Mexico. Now theory would have to be tested.

My playhouse was not a great laboratory. Nor was I some sort of scientist. James, by sheer luck or audacity, had developed a technology far beyond what was now known. He had conquered gravity. That knowledge alone put him in a league all by himself. His association with me, had made me, the possessor of that knowledge.

What was I to do with that knowledge? I was raised in church, by my grandparents. I had been a Bible reader and practitioner of my faith, from my youth. I was very well aware of the Biblical concept of, "To those, that much is given, much is required." I now possessed knowledge no man on earth, as far as I could know possessed. I didn't intend to take my position and responsibility lightly.

Maybe Margaret was right? Maybe the saucer was evil. Maybe it had possessed James. It certainly now possessed me. What about Margaret's concern for her children?

Unexpectedly one evening my phone rang, it was Mattie.

"Misser Boss, I just seen a thing on the T.V. about a UFO," after a long silence, "Uh, what do you know about that?" Mattie asked.

"Oh, I hear such things crop up, now and then," I said.

"Misser Boss, uh, what I really want to know, is what you know, about this exact one. You know this one?" Mattie asked.

"Mattie," I asked, "what did your mother have to say about the saucer sighting?"

"I haven't talked to her," Mattie said, "what's she got to do with flying saucers?" After a pause, "your right, maybe I better to talk to her. Misser Boss, can I come out to your place after I get off work?" Mattie asked.

"Why sure, you're welcome out here, but Mattie, talk to your mother first," I said.

"I'll come out this evening," Mattie said.

It was rather late when I saw the headlights coming up the driveway. I turned the porch light on and scolded my dog. "Get out and come in," I said.

It was Mattie and Margaret. "Mama said it was about time she came to see you," Mattie said.

I had known Margaret, nearly thirty years. This was the first time she had been to my house. Occasionally, I would run across her, usually with her mother, in town or some place. We talked by phone occasionally, but she rarely left her home. She never seemed at ease when I saw her in public. When I made visits to her home, she was always cordial. Even her father, Robert Green, had mentioned to me how she stayed home and rarely went out. Robert had died some time ago, for me it was a real personal loss. Old friends can't be replaced, especially old "Mis Fits."

"Well, this is a real surprise," I said to Margaret, "I didn't expect you."

"I'm sorry for barging in, but Mattie insisted I come. I guess I do need to get out of the house. I wanted – I – wanted, uh – I guess I need out of the house," Margaret stammered.

"Can mama see your saucer?" Mattie piped up.

"If she wants to," I said, "I'll be glad to show it to her."

"Yes," Margaret said, "I'd like to see that evil thing."

"Mama, it's not evil. It's a machine, like, like, a car or air-plane. It's a machine, nothing else." Mattie said.

"Machines scare me," Margaret said, "back when I worked at the factory, machines scared me. That's why your daddy took up with me. I was scared of the machines. Your daddy tried to protect me. I thought he was so sweet."

"Mama! You're embarrassing me and Missed Boss, too!" Mattie said.

"This is not embarrassing to me," I said, smiling "as a matter of fact, I've heard this story before, James' version. Mattie, I got to dance at your mother and daddy's wedding."

"Well, they never talked about such stuff," Mattie said, "I don't think I ever heard daddy talk much at all. Even to mama,"

"He didn't need to talk to me," Margaret said. "He said all he needed to say."

"Well, why not?" Mattie said, "Don't all men talk all the time?"

At last Margaret said, "Mr. Boss, can you explain this to Mattie? I'm at a loss for words."

"I don't think so," I said smiling. "Some things don't need explaining, at least by me. Let's go look at a machine."

As we walked out to my playhouse I said to Margaret, "I'm glad you decided to come for a visit. I was afraid you wouldn't come," I said.

"Maybe I do need to see that thing. I saw James when he was building his. I saw him drag it out of the barn, and I saw him take off in it. I was so relieved when he came back. After he came back, I saw him drag it back into the barn. When he came to the house for supper, he said he had been to your house. He was so excited. 'Maybe Mr. Boss can say words. I showed Boss, gravitron, Boss say words. I find way, Boss say the words.' I'm scared of those words," Margaret said.

I opened the door and turned the light on. Mattie headed for the addition door, then found her way through the door, and turned the lights on. "See mama, here it is, it's a machine like I told you. It's a flying machine. I think this is that UFO they reported on T.V., they acted like it was a joke or something. Then they started making wise cracks about a UFO story in 1984," Mattie said.

"Mattie, we've been down this road before," Margaret said. "So has Mister Boss. I don't want to go down it again."

"Well I'd like to ride in it. It flies now don't it?" said my friend Mattie.

"Yes, Mattie, it flies." Margaret said.

"How do you know it flies?" Mattie demanded of her mother.

"Mattie, I've known for two years. I didn't want you to know." Margaret said.

"Well, why not? If you knew, why didn't you tell me? Two years! You knew two years ago?" Mattie said, confused, "two years?"

"Margaret," I said, after Mattie became silent "Would you like to see a little demonstration?"

"That's what I came for," Margaret said.

"Mattie," I said, "let's go in the other room, turn the lights off and close the door."

"What kind of demonstration is mama going to see?" Mattie asked.

"Let's watch and see," I said.

I turned the big screen T.V. on in my play house, and then I installed a disk in my machine that looked like a VCR with several buttons. I punched the proper buttons. After a few seconds the T.V. came to life. The roof in the addition began to open, and the stars began to appear. Soon the image on the T.V. began to display a recognizable image. My house began to appear, and then fade into the distance. Soon a new image appeared, it was the James' house and property. At last there was the front door with a terrified dog, bristled up and yapping away.

"My, My, My," Margaret said. "How'd you do that?"

"Drone technology, incorporated in James' saucer." I said, as I pushed another button. It will be back in about ten minutes." We watched the T.V., there was the town we knew in the distance. Soon the saucer was back home and we heard the roof panels close. "We'll have to wait a few minutes before we can go back in. Zeta radiation, it will dissipate soon." I said.

"I thought it was a people saucer," at last Mattie said. "It's a robot."

"Mattie, it's a robot now. It was a people machine first, but it was too dangerous. This machine made its maiden flight with me in control. It's still a people saucer."

"Mama," as last Mattie said, "you and Mr. Boss know a lot more about a lot of things I don't, including this saucer. Mama you know a lot more about this saucer thing than David and I do, don't you? Does David know about this robot too?"

"Not yet," Margaret said, "I'll tell him when the time comes. That's after my grandchild gets here. You can keep quiet that long, can't you? At least two weeks?"

"You mean David's having a baby? I didn't know that either. I must live in a vacuum," Mattie said.

"I've had the same thing said about me, more than once," I said, smiling.

"Mattie, take me home, we've bothered Mr. Boss long enough for one day."

"You're no bother, come back anytime," I said.

"I'll be back, you can count on it," Mattie said. "Mama

we've got to talk!"

"I was afraid that day would come," Margaret said. "Thanks for your companionship over the years, for me and my family."

A few days later, Margaret called, "Mattie and I have been in Tulsa, I've got a new grandson."

"Well congratulations!" I said, "That first grandchild is rather special."

"Mr. Boss." Margaret said, "You're a Godfather. Now they named the baby after you. They're going to call him Boss."

"Well, I'm honored," I said, "when do I get to see him?"

"It won't be long, Mattie spilled the beans. Now David knows. We were watching the news and they said there had been a recent sighting of a UFO. She piped up 'Mr. Boss is making news again.'"

"What do you mean again?" David wanted to know. "Mattie, what do you mean again?"

"Mama, you got to tell him, I'm in trouble," Mattie said.

"You certainly are young lady," Margaret told Mattie. "Now David can't wait to fly around in that thing, at least, he's more responsible than Mattie. At least, I hope he is. I just don't know how to cope with anything, anymore. They've got their heads set on that evil machine. James has been gone seventeen years. Now all my fears have returned," Margaret said, sobbing.

"Margaret," I said, "this is really important. Do you want me to send this machine into outer space? I can if you say so."

After a long pause, "They've got their hearts set on that machine now. I just couldn't do that to them. I wish they had never heard of a flying saucer. They might have had a normal life. Their whole lives have been wrapped up in a space ship. I can't stand the thought they might not come back," Margaret said.

"Margaret, I can send it to outer space with my notes, that would be the end of it. That's an option," I said.

"They would never forgive me. I'd never forgive myself. You'd probably never forgive me either. What's worse, James would never forgive me. I guess, I'll just have to accept this," she said.

"Not if I send this thing to outer space," I said.

"No – Not now," Margaret said.

CHAPTER TWENTY-FOUR
ROBOT

There were real limits to the robots controls I had installed in the saucer. I had calculated that maybe fifty miles was the maximum range of the robot. Anything more would demand a human pilot, and the navigation was mostly line of sight. Flying a flying saucer by the seat of your pants was not a good way of flying a saucer. At slow speed and a low altitude, you could do well, but at higher speeds, things became a blur. The top speed at high altitudes could be measured in miles per second, not miles per hour. It became evident that the saucer could perform better at high altitudes. But the capsule was really limited in how high you could go. High speed at low altitude was severely limited. Not by the saucer, but by the pilot. The dissipation of heat generated by friction in the air, becomes a larger problem with increased speeds at low altitudes. With high speeds, you could become a fried chicken. The gravitron metal dissipates heat very well, but the salvaged airplane parts don't.

As I pointed out to James, he had built a Wright Brothers aircraft that could fly a thousand miles per hour. Maybe my saucer was a step up from James'. But it was not capable of miles per second, especially at low altitudes. The dynamics of saucer flight and spaceships are unlimited. There was no hard data available, only speculation and theories. Now I had to deal with the realities of saucer flight.

It didn't take a rocket scientist to figure out that saucer flight was a monster that eats people. The saucer technology had been developed by a factory worker, not a rocket scientist. My credentials were as a factory worker and a home builder, turned saucer builder. I had just created a bigger monster, to me, that was obvious.

When David and Mattie came out to my house, they had their hearts set on a flight in the saucer. But there was a danger I hadn't brought up. When I had built my saucer, I was aware of what had gone wrong with James' saucer. When James had brought his saucer out to my house, I asked him about Zeta radiation.

"You say words in dictionary" was James explanation.

"James," I asked, "What about Zeta? Have you taken precautions?"

"You say words," James said.

I now knew the words, but should I say them to James' family?

Margaret was sure the saucer was evil. Now, with what I had known for quite some time, there was something evil. I knew what it was...ZETA.

The higher the speed, the higher the exposure rate. ZETA dissipated quickly, but prolonged exposure was fatal. It's like a microwave. It cooks from the inside out. Once the damage is done, death follows quickly. James had taken several trips in his saucer at high speed, without giving consideration to ZETA. By choice, or by accident, the results were the same. James was going to die soon, that he knew. That explosion in James' barn was no accident. To spare his family, he energized his saucer, without control. He did not come back. Nor did he contaminate those he loved with ZETA.

Margaret knew the truth, as did I. Or at least we made a very accurate guess. When I began to unravel James' mystery, it became apparent what had happened.

"Mr. Boss," Margaret said, "We're going to have to tell my children what happened to their daddy, to keep them out of that saucer. It's just too dangerous."

"I agree," I said, "you want me to send it out?"

"Not yet. Let me talk to the kids first. We'll be out to your house this evening, if that's alright."

"I'll be waiting," I said.

CHAPTER TWENTY-FIVE
NO MORE - NO MORE

"**I**s that ZETA stuff why you made the saucer a robot?" Mattie asked.

"That's it," I said, "ZETA is lethal at high speed. There is no protection from ZETA when you crank this thing up at low altitude, the higher the speed the more ZETA radiation."

After a few moments, David asked "Is that exposure what made daddy take off in his machine?"

"Yes," I said, "James had been flying at high speed without protection. Outside of a lead suit, there's not much you can do but don't get exposed."

"Is it safe at slow speed?" Mattie wanted to know.

"I think so," I said, "but I wouldn't want to try it, without a better idea what we're up against. ZETA was produced by fast flying machines for many years. It caused several fatalities when machines became capable of supersonic flight. Blue eye protection and limited exposure time reduced the danger to near zero. But aircraft, even today's aircraft, can't fly at the speed that saucer can. Nor can airplanes reach the altitude the saucer can go."

"Well," David asked, "why did you build that thing, if you knew the danger?"

"ZETA is produced by friction in the atmosphere. Out of the atmosphere, ZETA is not produced. But the transition from atmosphere to space is not beyond the capabilities of this machine. It wasn't until I flew this thing by remote control, that I knew how dangerous ZETA is. Now I know and I appreciate its danger. Any human being flying at low altitudes, at high speed, is going to die. Die a horrible death," I said.

David asked, "How fast can this thing be flown safely, at low altitude?"

"About the speed of sound, at low altitudes, under about thirty thousand feet. Even that is courting disaster. These salvaged airplane parts are suspect."

"I want to fly it," David said, "if you say its safe."

"I think it's safe at slow speeds," I said. "I'm not afraid of it, but you'll have to talk to your mother."

"Mama," Mattie said, "please let me fly it."

"A saucer killed your daddy, and this thing will kill you," Margaret said.

"But mama, it's just a machine. Mr. Boss said it was safe at slow speeds. I want to fly in it," Mattie pleaded.

"Mama, I want to fly in it too," David said, "daddy wanted us to know about saucers, or he wouldn't have wanted Mr. Boss to say words."

"But it scares me," Margaret said. "I'd rather it took off and didn't come back, before it kills someone else dear to me."

"Mama, we're grown now, we can make our own decisions," Mattie said. "Isn't that right David?"

"Yes," David said, "but I have a family to consider now. I don't intend to take great chances."

"I've studied daddy's books, and I know what ZETA is, and what the dangers are. So does Mr. Boss. But the potential of saucers, far outweigh the obvious danger. That's something daddy knew. That's what Mr. Boss knows. And, that's what I know."

"But you don't know anything except a good time," David said to Mattie.

"Children," Margaret scolded, "don't start a fight. Mr. Boss and I have talked at great length about this machine. It scares me, but I also know what my husband, your daddy wanted. Your daddy wanted you to know the truth. The truth took his life, but he didn't want his children to die chasing his dreams. This thing is just too dangerous, it's evil!"

Mattie, David and I had all taken low altitude flights in the saucer, over the objections of Margaret. She still wanted me to send it to outer space. What concerned me was Mattie. She insisted on pushing the limits I set for her. It seemed a UFO had encountered an Air Force jet at sixty thousand feet, and sped off. The pilot reported such encounters were rare, but not unheard of. Astronauts had reported such encounters in the past.

"Mattie," I said, "what were you doing at sixty thousand feet? If that cabin pressure had failed, you'd be dead."

"I was careful," Mattie said, "see my ZETA monitor is still yellow."

"We're not talking ZETA here, we're talking cabin pressure," I said. "Mattie, you got to quit doing these things. Quit taking chances. That machine is not safe at sixty thousand feet. David, that's your sister, you talk to her. She's nuts!"

"I've known that since we were little kids," David said, sarcastically. "She's NUTS!"

Sometime later, David was analyzing the flight recorder on Mattie's last flight. "Mr. Boss, we got a problem."

"What kind of problem?" I asked.

"The 315 metal is showing signs of breaking down its reversing back to aluminum." David said.

"The party's over," I said. "Let's send this saucer to outer space, while we can. That will make Margaret happy."

I programed the saucer and pushed the button. The overhead panels opened, and then closed. There was an eerie green glow that soon subsided. "Well, it was fun while it lasted," I said. "At least your mama will be happy."

"Misser Boss, are you going to build another one?" Mattie asked.

"Nope, I'm just too old. I aim to retire again, and just vegetate. I had my run on the wild side, years ago," I said.

"But, Misser Boss, nobody but you knows how to build another saucer," Mattie pointed out.

"It's up to you kids now. I'm done. It's time for me to fade into the sunset and take my ailing wife somewhere peaceful and quiet, so we can live out our old age in peace."

PART THREE
Mr. Boss

CHAPTER TWENTY-SIX

NO MORE

T here is a real sadness that creeps into your heart when you've done your best – games over, you lose!

Sending the saucer into outer space was the climax of many years of painstaking work. But like all good things, eventually – they must end.

Margaret was thankful, - that evil machine was no more. David was understanding, and resolved to the fact more work was needed. And Mattie, - oh well! Now me, - my world was about to fall off its axis, - for personal reasons.

In the summer of 2005 I retired again. – No more saucers. I gave my notes on the gravitron to Margaret. It had taken me fifteen years to unravel James's secret, and another five to build the saucer.

The three years of the saucers existence, was the fulfillment of James's accomplishments. But again, - the saucer, – "Won't come back!"

James's family was now in possession of James's secret. – As far as I was concerned, - the secrets of space travel and James's departure belonged to them.

My wife, - the love of my life, was terminally ill. On the

best medical advise available, - we moved to central New Mexico, near the Rio Grande River. In what seemed an instant, to me, the disease ran its course. Now I was alone - my children, grandchildren, great-grandchildren and many longtime friends were 700 miles from me.

As a youth and young man I had spent considerable time in New Mexico. Even back then, I enjoyed my occasional long walks in the desert. Now, with my wife deceased and buried, long walks in the desert became almost a daily occurrence. Unless church work or volunteer work filled my days.

In my old age, now alone, from time to time, the ghost of my past would arrive – unannounced. How many times, I had dodged the bullet's headed my way – some real – some phantoms. The number of times, over my long life, I had been in the right place at the right time, with the right stuff, defied give common sense. All I could do was bow my head and give thanks to my God.

This place, my wife and I bought and named Rattlesnake Gulch, was one of those, unexplained paradoxes. Within a week after buying this place, we discovered we now live in the middle of what was the Camino Real, that ancient highway between Mexico City and Santa Fe, and that in my backyard, we had the site of at least three ancient civilizations. Within walking distance, were several more ancient sites for me to explore.

"The Trinity site," where the first nuclear explosion on earth took place, was about 30 miles away. Several of the best documented UFO encounters had taken place near the Trinity site. Roswell, San Antonio, Socorro, San Augustine Flats and others had taken place in the surrounding area. As I learned, supposedly, alien encounters had taken place out in the nearby deserts.

The alien encounters I had heard about, I met a certain amount of skepticism. Where was the proof? There was lots of hearsay – I took such hearsay with a grain of salt.

As a young lad I had been a state finalist in the science fair. And as a young man, an Army veteran, I had worked at White Sands and been a student at New Mexico State. But personal obligations brought me back to my roots in Oklahoma, and my eventual association with James.

Not long after my wife and I had taken up residence in New Mexico, I got a call from Margaret.

"Mr. Boss," said Margaret. "David has gone to work in Houston, doing something. He knows I have your notes, I don't know what to do. David said those notes would be a great help to him in his job. I'm afraid David and maybe Mattie too are messing with saucers again."

"Maybe, I should have sent those notes into space too," I said.

"My children . . ." Said Margaret, between the sniffles. "That saucer possessed James . . . It took him . . . Now it's getting my children . . . I'm afraid of those evil machines!

"I'm sorry," said Margaret, "I called to see if you had any objections if I let David have your notes, – not complain about my fears. That's all your notes!"

"Margaret, that was James's work, I just translated his work into English. That work belongs to James and his family, not me. James left the world his blueprints. Somehow, for some reason, James trusted me to say words. Like all men, he wanted his children to appreciate his life's work. Not much more in this life is worthwhile."

"I'm afraid," said Margaret. "James wasn't afraid, you're not afraid, my children are not afraid . . ."

"Margaret you could burn those notes, – with my blessing," I said.

"I can't do that," said Margaret, between sobs. "My children would never forgive me. Their daddy would never forgive me."

"Margaret, David is a very responsible young man. – With the family of his own, he's not going to take any unnecessary chances, and Mattie, – she's not afraid of anything, – even the unknown," I said. "I wish I could be of more help."

"Mr. boss," said Margaret. "You and your wife have been more help to me and my children than you'll ever know. Your wife and I shared many of the same fears, – flying saucers. They took our husbands.

CHAPTER TWENTY-SEVEN
DUDES

My wife had been gone quite some time, and I had settled into some semblance of a human-being again. My long walks in the desert was now a common occurrence.

Old man, with not much else to do, sometimes, embark on the development of a hobby, – at least I did. Some time ago, before my wife died, somehow, someway, I became fascinated with ancient cultures and their tool making. No piece of flint, chert, obsidian, was safe from me. I learned to turn rocks into stone tools, – in the traditional way. Probably only old dinosaurs develop an interest in ancient technology. My stone tool making hobby became a hobby out of control. I started putting my creations in shadow boxes, and giving them to anyone that would take one.

The surrounding desert provided an ample supply of stones to make arrowheads, fishhooks, knives, scrapers, and 'things' out of. A good distance from my home, there is ravine where ancient peoples once dwelled, and left evidence of their existence. Also that ravine was a good source of rock, suitable for 'knapping.' (That's making stone tools, in the traditional way. Not, taken an afternoon siesta!) At my age, I do both!

Now I'm a long-long way from nowhere with my nose

pointed toward my toes, looking for suitable rocks for knapping. Usually I carry my knapping tool with me, on these rock hunts. When I find a promising rock, I would take my hammer stone, 'flake a chip,' and give it a try. If it was worthy, I put the rock in my sack and toted it the long way back home. Rocks are heavy. – They get real heavy, on long walks.

I had found a couple of worthy stones. I was near the ravine I had hunted several times before. I was trying to find a good place to descend the steep incline to the canyon's floor. Off in the distance, I see this 'dude' down on his hands and knees, digging in the dirt.

"Well now," I said to myself. *"Where did that stray cat come from, and how did he get here?"* The nearest road, within 20 miles, ends at my house, – that's six or seven miles from here. And I ain't seen no Jeep, horse, or jackass and rider, go by my house in a Coons age.

Now I stood there looking down at that dude, trying to figure him out. First off, he was wearing pink, – and – he's got a pink bonnet on for a hat. He's got an open pink suitcase and a pink pole lying on the ground nearby.

Now old, retired, transplanted Okie's, just don't expect to encounter such sights out in the desert!

Now this 'dude' seems to be occupied scratching in the dirt. I'm kind of thinking – *old age is finally got me, I'm seeing things!*

I made my way down the steep incline, walked the short distance to where the dude is.

"Howdy," I say, holding my hoe in my left hand and lifting my right hand in a greeting.

That strange dude unravels! In an instant, that cat is on his feet, that pink pole is pointing at me, and his eyes, under that pink bonnet are about to pop out of his head!

This encounter has left me a little unnerved.

"Howdy," I says, "didn't aim to scare you."

This dude just held his ground, pointing his pink stick at me. After a while, he retrieves, what I think is a cell phone from his belt. He kinda holds it up as if taking my picture, and starts jabbering in some kind of gibberish I ain't never heard before.

"Sorry, didn't aim to scare you," I said.

After another jabber, he lays his pink pole down, puts his cell phone back on his belt, and lifts his hand in what I take as a howdy greeting.

Now I'm an old Okie, and everyone that knows me, knows I'm kind of jumpy. This strange dude has my undivided attention. I was kinda thinking of leaving and going back home. He just didn't seem too friendly.

I'm just standing there. Wondering what to do next when this dude gives me a wave that I take as 'come on down.' All the time, pointing at his pink suitcase.

Now I am kind of a curious fellow. I'd sort of wondered what he was up to, – maybe pink is what archaeologist wear these days? – We were not far from an ancient campsite.

Now this dude starts his show and tell, he shows me a small clear container, there is some dirt, another with rocks, and another – could that be a lizard?

Not to be outdone, I sat down on a rock, opened my sack and retrieved a rock and handed it to the dude. By his looks, I interpreted as utter confusion, he hands me my rock back after a careful examination.

Now I had his attention I now took my hammer stone, after a careful examination, I hit the rock and a chip came off suitable for an arrowhead. In short order, I took my flaking tool and began to shape the chip. After fluting, I had created a decent looking arrowhead.

When I handed it to the 'dude,' I thought his big clear eyes would explode after turning green! He opened an empty vile and put my arrowhead in his suitcase.

I noticed while I was flaking the chip, the dude cell phone was in operation and somebody, somewhere was getting an ear and eye full.

After show and tell, I decided to go back home, – I pointed toward my house and did a walking motion with my fingers.

After waving my goodbyes, I turned around and started to climb out of the ravine. After my exhaustive climb, for an old man, there at the top stood that dude in the pink bonnet, his pink pole was in one hand and his pink suitcase was in the other.

"How'd he do that?" I wondered. *"Maybe I'm getting old?"*

Now, I take the long stroll back across country to my house, and this dude keeps in step. I didn't know, company was coming to my house.

When I get to my front door, this strange dude seems to get a little edgy. I opened the door, but this dude sits his suitcase down, he clutches his pink pole with both hands, and gingerly enters my front door. Real cautious like, he surveys his new surroundings . . . when – all at once – my cuckoo clock starts to cuckoo. In an instant, that dude pointed his stick – my clock stops – and the pendulum is stationary, – pointing left. Now this ninja warrior with his pink stick just killed my cuckoo clock. When the chiming clock on my mantle set off, old pink bonnet pointed his stick at it – but he let it live. When the chiming subsided pink bonnet pointed his pink stick at my cuckoo clock, – it began to– cuckoo, – and it had lost six hours in an instant. –

That pink stick now had my attention!

In the batting of an eye, pink bonnet looked at me, seemingly confused. Abruptly, he turned around, walks through the door, picks up his pink suitcase, and marches out of my front gate, across country, and vanished out of my sight, back the way we came.

I knew, – right off, – dudes wearing pink bonnets, – carrying pink sticks, – didn't come from around here.

CHAPTER TWENTY-EIGHT
ANOTHER ARROWHEAD

T ime flies when you're having fun. – It drags by when you just exist. I guess it was a month or two later, rather early in the morning, when, for a moment, I think I see something, falling earthward, leaving an ever so faint vapor trail. – 'Is that green?' I wondered.

"*Now that's odd,*" I says to myself. "*Maybe I'm seeing things.*" From my perspective, on my front porch, it looked like the little 'something' came down in the general area where I had encountered that strange dude dressed in pink, carrying that pink stick, sometime back.

I had seen similar sites, as a young man. Just out of the Army, I was able to go to work at White Sands. At the time, missiles were being fired from Fort Wingate, near Gallup, New Mexico, and crash landed on White Sands proving grounds. Telemetry data was then collected, analyzed, and interpreted for the next shot. Occasionally things didn't go exactly as planned, as anyone out here knew. One or two of those shots that went awry caused a little excitement. They were flying objects quickly identified. There were however, flying objects around, not identified.

As close as I now lived to the north end of White Sands Missile Range, or proving ground, – or whatever they call it these days. Now in my old age, I just half way, expected to see things in the sky I couldn't identify. After all, it had been over fifty years since I worked at White Sands.

It seemed to me, a good day for a long rock hunt. I hadn't been back to the ravine where I had run into pink bonnet. It took me several hours to meander to the ravine. From a high point, where I stood, there was nothing to see. I carefully picked my way down to the floor of the ravine and continued my rock hunt.

I had been in this ravine several times. At the west end, of the ravine, where I had entered the ravine, the sand delta was a half mile wide. A couple miles on West was the Rio Grande River. East, up the ravine, the delta narrowed, the wall on each side became higher and steeper, and at the terminal end East, was what would pass for a waterfall, – with no water. Where I had encountered pink bonnet was somewhere near that waterfall.

I had decided to meander up east toward the waterfall. That was probably a mile walk, about halfway to the waterfall. I came upon some footprints in the sand, in a rather broad expanse.

You can tell a lot about footprints in the sand, either man or beast, if you're familiar with your surroundings. Cat tracks, by the size, you know if it's a skunk, bobcat, or a cougar. Dog tracks, maybe wolves or coyotes. Hoof prints are deer, havalina, oryx, elk or cows. – Never had I seen, people prints in this ravine. – But there they were. – And – they just didn't look right. I had never seen a human shoe print like that.

I decided to follow the footprints South. – They just ended. There were some large indentations in the sand, but nothing else I could see. "*That's odd,*" I said to myself.

After my exploration down south, I followed the tracks north. They just went up to the rock wall and stopped. It looked

D.W. SMITH

like those tracks walked through the rock! *"Okay,"* I says to self, – *"Now you're seeing things. - That can't be! Maybe I should stay out of the desert!"*

I was certainly no closer to unraveling the mysterious footprints in the sand, so I continued my rock hunt. I found a nice rock to test for my arrowhead making. I sat down on a nearby rock opened up my sack, got my tools out, and a bottle of water, and set about testing my rock. After the rock whop, and retrieving the chip, I loosened the cap on my water bottle and took a big swig. – Out of the corner of my eye, I see this dude, – in a pink suit, pointing a pink stick at me!

Now I had seen a dude in a pink suit kill a cuckoo clock sometime back. – I didn't figure that pink stick would do me any good either.

"Howdy," says me. "I didn't see you coming." I raised my hand as a greeting.

Now this dude goes for his belt, gets his cell phone, takes my picture and starts jabbering a mile a minute.

I just sat there. In an instant this dude puts his cell phone back on his belt, lowers his pink pole and marches over to me. He just stands there and stares pointing at my hands.

Now I'm old, I've been in the Army, I've been shot at, – I drove racecars for years and I've even taken several joyrides in a homemade lying saucer. Not much bothers me – except, dudes in pink suits, wearing bonnets, and pointing pink sticks at me. This dude's bonnet is yellow.

In my state of utter bewilderment, I think to myself, *"surely archaeologists don't all where pink suits and were bonnets, – pink or yellow!"*

Not knowing what else to do, I take my flaking tool, and start shaping an arrowhead. After fluting my creation, I handed it to the dude seeming transfixed at my handiwork. That was the second time I saw clear eyes turn green.

Now this rock I had been sitting on was getting hard on my butt. After gathering up my tools and rock and taking another swig of my water, I stood up. Using my hoe handle as a butt jack, after looking around – that dude ain't nowhere in sight! Now I was out another arrowhead.

Yep, I've been out in the desert sun too long. – I must be seeing things!

Not long after my wife and I moved to Rattlesnake Gulch, we were sitting out on our porch enjoying the cool desert evening. We sat there some time, talking, holding hands, and occasionally swatting a mosquito, when off in the distance we see this light, kinda trickling down from the sky. It seemed to fall end over end, – stay stationary, – and then fell end over end. Eventually it seemed to come to earth not too far away.

"Maybe we should call someone," I said.

"I'll call 911," said my wife.

Soon she returned, sat down really close to me, "the 911 operator asked if I was new around here?" Said my wife.

When you've been married to a woman as long as I have, you just know when things don't set well with her.

"I think I'll go call Dorothy," said my wife. Dorothy was her new friend in our new church.

Soon my little wife returned to my side. – The silence was deafening. – "Dorothy said it was probably aliens. – Somebody is always running upon them, – out in your neighborhood."

The thought occurred to me, *"we may be on our way back to Oklahoma,"* she never was too keen on flying saucers.

CHAPTER TWENTY-NINE
GIFTS

Twice, a couple of years ago I had come upon, dudes in pink tights wearing bonnets. I had no idea who they were or where they came from. Maybe it was their strange appearance, – 'space men?'

"Could it be possible?" I wondered.

I had no doubt space travel was a real possibility, even for us, in the near future. Thanks to James, the direction was clear. Antigravity devices would make it possible, – in the near future.

I had followed James's blueprints, and built a crude saucer. I had pushed my limits of understanding. It was time for me to step back and let younger men step up. – No one confused Mattie McFeen with being a man, she was as pretty as she was talented

David McFeen was conscientious, cautious, resourceful, calculating and deliberate. But Mattie, – hardheaded, – unafraid and determined is about all I could say with surety.

When my wife and I moved to New Mexico, the only occasion I had to hear about the McFeen kids, – those rare occasions, were talks I had with Margaret.

As my wife's health deteriorated, I knew less and less of

the McFeens. Distance, and other concerns, governed my day to day existence. Robert Greene, Margaret's elderly fathers health was failing as my wife's. – Our children were about the business of establishing their own way in the world. The last I knew, the McFeen kids, David and Mattie were doing something in Houston, Texas. Margaret was terrified her children were involved with those evil saucers again. The only explanations they gave was, 'classified research.'

The desert monsoon had come again and stayed kinda late this year. It had rained, and the sand piles, were somewhat stable. I decided to take a chance and drive my old truck down the cow trails to the ravine where I had encountered those strange fellows. Without moisture, sand is impossible. – You can bury up to your axles and stay there until the next monsoon.

I picked my way around the chollas and mesquites, to the ravine. I parked my truck, got my rock sack, water, hoe and started my rock hunt. About noon or so, I had gotten to the waterfall with no water, when I took note of my surroundings. I was at the base of a rock ledge. Standing atop, looking down at me were three dudes in pink tights. One was pink bonnet. The other two wore yellow bonnets. In an instant all three, jumped off that ledge, and were standing before me.

After a few moments of awkward silence pink bonnet, made a walking motion with his fingers and pointed toward my house.

In sign language, I made a driving motion and pointed toward my truck. Again, pink bonnet made a walking motion and pointed toward my house.

It took me a while, but I began to understand pink bonnet wanted to visit my house again. "*Why?*" I wondered.

I made my 'come on' motion, and started to walk toward my truck. Soon pink bonnet and one yellow bonnet were in step, marching by my side.

After the walk, we arrived at my truck. I pointed to the passenger side door. I opened the driver side door, and slid in. The dudes in pink stood there., inside I opened the passenger door. After deciding both things would not fit in the cab, both laid their pink poles in the back.

When I started the truck, both dudes tried to get out but they didn't know how to open the door. After considerable hand motions and assurance, both dudes settled down somewhat. My old truck has a standard floor shift. Both foreigners seem to be awestruck, by my gear shifting and clutch action. Soon both got out their cell phones, one seemed to record my foot action, and the other my hand actions. The engine noise and the driving actions seem to be of great interest to the strangers.

When we arrived home, I parked in front of my house both men, – if they were men, – sat seemingly confused as to what to do next. I reached across both men jammed next to the door, and open the door. Both were out in an instant.

Yellow bonnet, now out of my truck, headed for his pole. After looking at pink bonnet, and a jabbering contest, yellow bonnet laid his pink pole back in my truck.

I gave them my 'come on in' motion. Yellow bonnet was quite hesitant to enter my front door. He seemed to be unsure of himself. After a look at pink bonnet, and another jabbering contest, yellow bonnet came on in.

The strangers stood there surveying their surroundings. At last pink bonnet pointed at my cuckoo clock, then he pointed at my mantel clock, soon both clocks began to note the hour. I could tell, yellow bonnet wanted to leave.

When the clock mystery ended both men began to take note, the Jack-a-lope over my mantel clock seemed to be quite fascinating, as did my two guitars. Maybe a musical demonstration was in order.

I picked up one of my guitars, sat down on the couch, and began to strum the instrument. Both sets of clear eyes turned green! The cell phones were now out and the jabbering and picture taking began again.

Seemingly transfixed, pink bonnet dared to touch the guitar.

I took my finger, pressed one string, and plucked the strain. Then I moved my finger up the string changing the pitch. After demonstrating chord changes, and playing a short medley, I handed the instrument to pink bonnet.

If the eyes are the windows of the soul, – now I was confused! Clear eyed, – pink bonnet just turned blue! – His whole face! Even more astonishing, the medley I played, pink bonnet played. – With my mistakes! All the time yellow bonnet is recording our concert.

There are some things you just can't explain. – All the stuff on my walls, defies explanation. – My late wife was a doo-dad collector, and whatever she collected got hung on a wall or put in a glass cabinet. – It is everywhere, – in every room.

After considerable time in my wife's junk room, I invited my guests, outback, to my junk room.

As we passed through the kitchen, I went to the refrigerator and took out three bottles of water. After I handed one to each of my guests, I unscrewed the cap and took a large gulp. My guests just stood there, holding the bottles.

At length, yellow bonnet retrieved a small vial from somewhere, unscrewed the cap, poured a few drops in the vial and both handed me my bottled water. I began to wonder what was wrong with my water.

We now continued through the kitchen, outback to my junk room. I guess my junk room is a travel to a different world. There is a wall covered with shadow boxes full of my stone creations. There are two tables stacked high with rock, and a chair setting between them, with debitage, rock chips and stone trash thrown about, on the floor.

On another wall, floor to ceiling, is shelves and cabinets full of exotic rock, handmade artifacts, guns, gun shell casings, bows and arrows, Tomahawks, stone knives, axes and more junk.

On another wall is a number of photographs. There are pictures of me, my wife, my children, my grandchildren, my racecars and homes I designed and built. – And more junk.

I sat down in my chair and began to give my guests another demonstration in stone tool-making, using different stone, of a different color and composition.

Yellow bonnet seemed to be taking considerable interest in my knapping. But pink bonnet is studying my photo collection. Collectively, I suppose, those photos are a capsule image of my long life.

One photo was rather recent of me and my wife, taken shortly before she died. Pink bonnet, seem to be spellbound, – he would look at the photo, – then it me. He'd look at another photo then at me.

After finishing my latest creation, I tried to explain the photo to my guests.

My mother kept a photo album of my growing up until her death. There were baby pictures, child pictures, teen pictures, adults in uniform, wedding pictures, etc.

I pointed at a baby picture, then it me, then at a kid picture, then it me, at last to the last photo in my mother's album, and then it me. The evidence of my aging process revealed in the photographs seemed to be spell binding to both aliens, as were the women.

When this latest show and tell was coming to an end, I took a couple of my shadow boxes of stone tools, a stone ask, knife and a photograph of me, by the side of my saucer creations. Of all the photographs on my wall, that was the one both strangers took pictures of with their cell phones.

In time I was to learn those cell phones, were crypt-a-cones. – That terminology was something approximating translation.

My guests, clutching their new gifts, rode in my old truck back to their delta. As they disembarked and retrieved there poles from the back of my truck, I pointed at them, after considerable motioning pink bonnet gave me a demonstration. A road runner was nearby. Pink bonnet pointed his pole and the road runner stopped, – dead in his tracks, – in mid-motion and just fell over. A few seconds later pink bonnet pointed his pole; the road runner came to life and continued on his path. – I was duly impressed.

While we were waving our goodbyes, I guess it was the first yellow bonnet I had encountered, from somewhere, appeared. He handed pink bonnet a small metal looking 'something.'

In an instant both yellow bonnets marched out of sight. Pink bonnet seemed to stare at me intently. At last, with his finger, he touched my forehead. The nearest I could describe the sensation was that of profound gratitude. Soon pink bonnet took the device, pointed at the scratches and circles on the end, then he made three distinct motions with his finger, – with that,

– pink bonnet handed me the metal 'something,' and followed his companions.

A few days later I took the metal 'something,' over to the local university. Their analysis was inconclusive. They offered to send it to another laboratory for more testing. After some six months, and considerable aggravation, the 'something,' was returned to me with the suggestion that I had, somehow, perpetrated a hoax!

CHAPTER THIRTY
CRYPT-A-CONE

I t had been some time, maybe a year since my last encounter with the 'dudes in pink.' Outside of their unusual attire, and facial features, they seem to be almost human.

In this age of kinky hairdos, outlandish dress, bodies covered in tattoos and body piercings, the 'dudes in pink,' appeared to be almost human.

Being somewhat skeptical of alien encounters, as reported by the news media, it was obvious even to me these dudes didn't come from earth. – I didn't know where they came from, but I was certain it wasn't from someplace nearby.

The three times I came across the strangers, it was in the same ravine, in about the same general location.

In the last year or so, I had made several pilgrimages to that ravine, but nothing unusual occurred. If it were not for the 'something,' I had been given; I would probably have relegated my alien encounters as figments of my imagination, due to my old age.

When the device was returned to me, I spent considerable time looking at the alien device. I was intently looking at the circles on the end of the 'something,' – in a fixed stare. Wondering, *"What in the world is this thing?"* – When, – in a few seconds, – in my head, – the answer appeared!

When things, – unexpected, – appear, – in your head, – you 'freak out,' – I closed my eyes in a panic, in utter confusion, – the image disappeared! My question had been answered. – *"This is a 'crypt-a-cone'."*

When reason, and sanity, returned to my unnerved existence, I recounted what had just happened.

I remembered pink bonnet had pointed at those circles, and made three distinct hand motions. Somewhat, uneasy and unnerved, I picked up the device, stared at the circles, and asked the question again, *"What is this?"* –Again, – the image appeared with the explanation, – this is a 'crypt-a-cone.' Again, I closed my eyes and looked away. – The image disappeared!

I began to ask sample, simple questions, – *"Where am I?"* – I saw me, sitting in my house, – in my junk room, – among my clutter, – staring at a 'crypt-a-cone!'

After numerous simple questions, I decided to ask, – *"What is the square root of two?"* The never ending cascade of numbers continued until I closed my eyes.

I soon learned not to ask some questions. The answers were beyond my understanding! There were some questions the 'crypt-a-cone' would not answer, but the multitude of questions it would answer was beyond my understanding. Sometimes there were a number of explanations, offered.

There were no words in my vocabulary, nor was there a translation into English, from the alien language of some explanations.

After much trial and error, I gained an understanding of the 'crypt-a-cone' and its use. The one answer I most desired was beyond my understanding. – *"Why was I entrusted with this device?"*

CHAPTER THIRTY-ONE
CRASH ENCOUNTER

I had gotten in the habit of looking off toward the south. Maybe it was the three encounters I had with the strangers. Three times, I had run upon those unusual beings. I chanced to be looking south, when a strange light seemed to divide and then kind of fall to earth haphazardly. The largest light seemed to come to earth somewhat east of my house, in the general direction of the Trinity site on the north end of White Sands.

Early the next morning shortly after daybreak, I got my hoe, water and rock sack, and took a long walk in the general direction of the falling light show. After I had made a long walk out and back across the rough terrain, I called the Sheriff's office.

Shortly after noon, two deputies were sent out to investigate. The deputies stopped at my house to get directions to the crash site. A couple of hours later the two deputies got in their squad car and headed back to town.

On the 5 o'clock evening news on the local radio station, was an item of local interest:

. . . Several local residents reported seeing an unusual light show south east of town . . . One resident of the area . . . A crash site, with victims . . . Two deputies investigated . . . Another alien encounter

hoax...

Late in the summer evening, nearing sundown, a reporter appeared on the old man's porch, identifying himself as a reporter for some news service unannounced. Soon his questions became an inquisition.

"Look Mr.," said the rude reporter, "I'm just trying to do my job. – That's all. – You reported several dead bodies, and a crashed alien spacecraft. – Now I want to know where they are at, – that's all! There's not anything out there! Not one scrap of evidence!"

"There was when I call the Sheriff's office," said the old man, pointing east. "That way, – six or seven miles!"

"I've been out there with those deputies," said the reporter annoyed. – "Why'd you call the Sheriff and report some dead bodies? There ain't nothing out there but sand, rocks, and lizards!"

After the heated interview, the old man's patience was about at an end. "Well," said the old man emphatically. "There was when I called the Sheriff's office. Now get off my porch!"

The reporter insisted, "I was out there with those deputies! There wasn't anything out there but dirt and cacti!"

"Now I've said all I'm going to say you, – except, – you get off my porch! – Get in your car and get off my place, before I decide to shoot your young ass!" Snapped the old man.

"Don't you threaten me!" Yelled the reporter.

"That wasn't a threat! That was a promise. You better be gone when I get back with my gun. – Now git!" Snarled the old man, slamming the door.

A couple of hours later, the two deputies came in the front gate, got out, and cautiously approached the old man's door.

"Can we talk to you?" Asked the deputy.

"We ain't got nothing to talk about," said the old man.

"That reporter filed a complaint. He said you threatened him. Is that so?" Asked the deputy.

"No! I didn't threaten him! I promised I'd shoot his ass if he didn't get off my porch. That's exactly what I meant! He had the good sense to get gone, before I got my gun."

"You got a gun?"

"You got a warrant?"

"I can get one."

"Maybe you need to go to town and get one," said the old man.

"Can we talk about this?" Asked the deputy.

"There ain't nothing to talk about. You're the two deputies they sent out to investigate. You're the ones that got this started," said the old man, then he added. "It was a three hour walk out there, and a three hour walk back. You jackasses was back in town in two hours."

"There wasn't anything out there," said the deputy.

"There was when I called the Sheriff's office," the old man restated.

"There wasn't anything out there. We walked around in the desert," said the deputy.

"There was when I call. You jackasses didn't walk very far in an hour, – did you?"

After the heated debate the old man was taken in for questioning.

"Why'd you call in a bogus report?" The Sheriff asked. "There wasn't anything out there."

"There was when I called you," said the old man. "Them jackass deputies didn't walk no five or six miles in rough country like I told them to. They was back in town drinking coffee in two hours or less."

"My deputies said they didn't find anything. – There wasn't anything to find," said the Sheriff. "How'd you know about those bodies?"

"I saw them. They were by the wreck," said the old man.

"What wreck? There wasn't any debris out there. The deputies searched the area. They didn't find any crash site," said the Sheriff.

"Them bozos couldn't find their ass with both hands," said the old man.

"You suppose you might be seeing things?"

"I know what I saw."

"How old are you?" The Sheriff asked.

"Seventy-eight. What's that got to do with dead bodies? I ain't dead yet."

"You live out there alone?"

"Yes. My wife died several years ago."

"I see. Would you submit to a medical examination?" The Sheriff asked.

"What for? I'm not sick. – I don't see things. – I don't tell lies. – I told you what I saw," the old man affirmed again.

"There wasn't anything out there. – At least the deputies didn't find anything," said the Sheriff.

After a lengthy questioning, the old man was allowed to go home. But he was admonished that further questioning might be necessary.

CHAPTER THIRTY-TWO
BODIES

E arly the next morning, a car drove up the old man's driveway. Two young men got out stepped up on the porch.

The old man opened the door, "I done told you what I saw. I ain't telling you again! Get off my porch!"

"Sir," one of the men said, showing his credentials and badge. "We're from the United States space agency. According to the wire service, a possible UFO sighting and crash site was reported. The local sheriff gave us your name, and resident location."

"We're not here to cause you any trouble! We're here to ask you if you could show us the location of the dead bodies, you saw. Would you be willing to show us the exact location?"

"Well now," said the old man, after a short discussion. "It's a long walk."

"We got a car," the man said.

"It won't help you. There ain't no road and its rough terrain. You fellers don't look like you're familiar with the desert and snakes. Not with them shining shoes and pretty clothes."

"We'll manage," said young man.

"If you young bucks think you're up to it, I'll get my hoe, we might see a snake. I'll get some water too, it's hot out there," said the old man.

When the old man returned with his hoe, and bottled water, the young men had shed their coats, donned straw hats, and walking boots. Each carried a small bag.

"Well now, that's quite a transformation," said the old man.

"We've been out on UFO hunts," one of the young men said.

As the men started their trek across country, one of the young men asked, "Sir, how close to those dead bodies did you get?"

"Maybe fifty feet. Close enough to see they were dead. I counted five scattered about, and their craft was in pieces."

"We read that report you gave the Sheriff. If you saw that light show, why was it the next day before you called in?" Asked the young man.

"You'll know by the time we get there and back."

The men had walked in rough terrain for over two hours, under a relentless desert sun.

"I'm beginning to get the picture," said the young man. "How much farther?"

"A couple of miles, I guess. It's all uphill. I need to sit a spell. I ain't as young as I used to be," said the old man.

The old man was getting his second wind, when one of those young men asked, "How did a man with your credentials wind up in a place like this?"

"My credentials?" Said the old man surprised. "I ain't got no credentials. My wife and I came out here to the high and dry to die. She got the job done, – I'm still here."

"Do these people out here know about you and your work?" Asked the young man.

"I hope not. There ain't nothing to know. I ain't working no more. I'm just too damned old, and to mad at half-witted reporters, and incompetent deputies, to talk to nitwits."

The men continued on. At last the men were topping a little rise, "We're about there," the old man said. Maybe the buzzards ain't got `um."

"Oh my God! It's true! It's an alien spacecraft." Said the young man identified as Shawn.

"It has to be!" Said Kevin, the other young man.

"I told them jackasses there was dead bodies. The buzzards ain't got them yet and there's that junkyard too," said the old man, smiling.

"How'd you find this crash site?" Asked Shawn.

"I been walking over this desert for seven years. There's a lot more than meets the untrained eye. Want me to help you fellers? Them aliens have landed here a bout's before," said the old man.

"Naw, we can take it from here," said one of the young man. "We've come prepared, – in case there was an alien crash site. You've been a great help. The nation thanks you for your service."

"Okay then," said the old man. "I think I'll go home. Can you young bucks find your way back to your car?"

"We can manage, – thanks again."

<><><><><>

The old man took the long hike back to his house. He set

about doing his daily chores as a bachelor with a household to run. After preparing his light lunch, he settled down in his recliner, to reflect on the day's events. Several hours later, well past sundown, he was awakened by the two young men knocking on his door.

"I see you made it back," the old man said. "I's afraid you'd get critter ate, or lost."

"Thanks again for your help," said Shawn. "Can we talk to you for a few minutes?"

"We're not recording, and hopefully we're not a nuisance," said Shawn.

"Well, come on in and sit a spell. I don't get much company out here. – Don't want much either," the old man added smiling. "Can I get you anything?"

"Water, maybe," said Shawn.

"You fellas ate today? I got sandwich stuff, if you're interested," offered the old man.

"Thanks for the offer, it's been a very long day," said Shawn.

"Sir," asked Kevin. "When did you know about that crash?"

"When I saw that streak of light, it was different. Their coming and goings don't usually look like that. When I saw that streak of light, I knew where they were headed. I had seen their comings and goings several times before. They leave a faint, short, light green trail."

"Do you know where they come from?" asked Kevin, looking at the old man intently.

"They're not from around here," said the old man, smiling. "I can tell you that."

"But, do you know where they came from?" Asked Shawn.

"Probably," said the old man. "They're not from around here."

"Sir," said Kevin. "A lot of people would like to know what you know. We were sent to ask you to cooperate. It's vital to our nation's security."

"And just when, by my God, did some jackass, somewhere, decide that!" The old man demanded.

"It became important when the local sheriff put your name on the Internet as a possible UFO witness. Your name got considerable attention in our agency." Said Kevin.

"After the grilling I got lately, you expect me to believe that?" The old man said.

"Sir, we've seen those reports you made over the years, since you've been out here in New Mexico. Some of those reports were hard to digest. But those dead bodies, puts things in a different light. Surely you understand that." Said Shawn.

"Uh Hu, I understand all right. And, I'm still mad as hell. You understand that, don't you?" Snarled the old man.

"Yes sir, I see how previous questions might leave you a little distraught. But sir, now, the nation needs your assistance. – Our nation needs to know what you know. We're asking for your cooperation." Said Shawn, respectfully.

"Uh Hu, well here is something for you to think about. Somebody let the cows out, now you're trying to get them back in the pasture, and close the gate. At least that's how I see it! You folks are a little late. Maybe five years. – Since I sent 'somebody' that 'crypt-a-cone'," said the old man.

"But there wasn't any proof, – just your word. Nothing we could verify. Surely, you understand. Now there's conclusive proof," said Shawn, apologizing.

"That 'crypt-a-cone' should have been proof enough," the old man pointed out.

The young men didn't have an answer. The old man seemed to be making his mind up. After a lengthy silence, looking at the young men he asked, "Those helicopters, I've seen buzzing around, – I take it, you removed the craft and bodies?"

"We're not authorized to divulge that information," said Shawn.

"Well, you damn well better get authorized! I'm not going to fool around with you nitwits very long, before I run you off and leave you on your own." Said the old man annoyed.

"Uh sir, can I use your phone? Asked Shawn.

"You mean in this modern age, you young bucks don't carry a cell phone?" Snarled the old man.

"Sir, on the chance your report was accurate, the danger was too great to have one on us. – Cell phones can be compromised. Surely you understand," said Shawn.

"The phone is in there," the old man said. "I ain't gonna wait all day."

In a few moments the young man returned after explaining his situation. Evidently there was some difficulty. The conversation ended with, "Yes sir, I don't see we have any choice."

When Shawn returned, he told Kevin, "the chief said to talk to this man, and answer any questions he might have."

"Well good," said the old man. "Let's start with something simple. Did you remove those bodies and spacecraft?"

"Why do you ask?" Asked Shawn.

"Now look turkey, I asked you a simple question. I'm not going to play twenty questions with you jackasses," snarled the old man.

"Uh yes, we removed them to a safe place," said Shawn.

"Well, here's the first pill you'd better swallow. Those folks are going to want their dead bodies and spacecraft back. My guess is, they will take them back, if they deem they need to." The old man pointed out.

"What makes you think they could do such a thing?" Asked Kevin.

"Well, let's see if you can get the gravity of the situation," said the old man. "Twelve men walked on the moon some fifty years ago and we and ain't been back. You just picked up five dead bodies and a junk spacecraft that arrived from millions of miles from here. And they've been running back and forth from here to Venus for centuries. Now, you made a little discovery. Has it occurred to you jackasses, you may be a little behind the times."

"Did you say they are from Venus? That's impossible! Venus is too hot for humans," said Kevin.

"And who said they were humans?" The old man asked.

"The medical team said they looked like humans, – well almost," Shawn admitted.

"So did Neanderthals, they looked like humans, – almost." The old man pointed out. "So do I, almost."

"You say you're not human?" One of the shocked young men asked.

"Not anymore, men have patience, mine's about gone," snapped the old man.

"I'm sorry sir but this is hard to contemplate," said Shawn.

"Not as hard as its going to be if you eggheads don't get out of the dark ages and science books. Maybe it's about time you eggheads start taking lessons, instead of giving them," the old man said. – Then he added, "When I sent that 'crypt-a-cone' to you people, five years ago, you didn't even try to turn it on. You ran chemical a analysis, you poured acid on it, you scratched it with diamonds, you hammered on it and tried to x-ray it, but, you didn't have sense enough to turn it on. 'Crypt-a-cone' is an alien communication device, and a whole lot more!"

"But the results came back inconclusive,, unidentified," said Kevin.

"Well, at least after I pitched a bitch, you jackasses returned it to me! You didn't know what it was anyway. You people called it – a something or another, – of an unknown material. And then you had the audacity to suggest that it was something I sent as a hoax, – like I was some kind of nut!"

"All I can say," said Shawn, looking at the floor. "Is our agency made an error in our analysis, and maybe our judgment."

"You bet your ass you made an error, and I pointed that out to you, in no uncertain terms! Ain't that in your report too?" demanded the old man.

"Uh, – yes sir, but it was hard to – to – you know – make sense of..."
"Make sense of," interrupted the old man. "Make sense of, – does anybody in that lab speak Okie English? All you need to do is follow the yellow brick road, it don't lead to Oz. It leads to our space!"

"Yes sir, we see that now," said Shawn apologizing.

"Well whoop-de-doo!" The old man said snarling. "The chickens have come home to roost, – maybe!"

CHAPTER THIRTY-THREE
GUESSWORK

There was a badly needed interlude of silence around the combatants. At last the old man asked, "Is there anyone with any sense in your agency?"

"Well," said Kevin. "There is a woman that has spoken of some man that worked with her dad years ago. When this crash issue came to light in our agency, she shocked everybody. She said, 'you better listen to that man.' She swears you're probably the man she knew as a young woman. Her position carries considerable weight. She heads the gravity research department. She sent us. She said we needed an education. Now we know what she meant."

"And just who might this young lass be?" The old man asked, smiling. "Or do I need to guess?"

"She said, "'Tell Misser Boss hi,' if we ran across him. Are you that Misser Boss?" Shawn asked.

"I've not answered to Misser Boss in years. How is Mattie? I heard she had moved up in the world. I knew she couldn't leave gravitron alone," said the old man smiling.

"Sir," said Shawn. "That's top-secret stuff."

"Not to me it ain't," said the old man. "And just what do

you young bucks know of antigravity propulsion anyway?"

"Uh, sir, not much, we're security investigators, you know possible security breaches," said Shawn. "That crash leaves a lot of unanswered questions obviously you know a lot more than we do. I'm beginning to understand a lot of things."

"Well now, that's kind of refreshing for a change. You young bucks may not be as dumb as you look," said the old man, smiling. – "By the way, is David up there too?"

"I don't understand. Which David? We have several." Said Shawn somewhat confused.

"David McFeen, Mattie's brother," affirmed the old man.

"I didn't know that David McFeen and Mattie McCullen were related," the stunned young man said.

"Well, what do you investigate?" The old man asked.

"Possible alien activity, we get numerous reports, but seldom any proof," said Shawn.

"Hogwash," the old man scoffed. "You've been getting proof since the Roswell thing in `47, I know for a fact."

"Sir," one of the young men said. "We have a lot of questions we need to ask. Will you cooperate?"

"You got any sense?" The old man asked.

"I'm beginning to wonder. This investigation is starting to get complicated. I don't know where to start," said Shawn, shaking his head.

"Let me help you out you're supposed to be asking about some dead bodies and a wreck. Ain't that right?" Said the old man.

"Yes sir," said Shawn.

"Well now, let me do a little guesswork." Said the old man. "That incoming ballistic missile, that somebody, somewhere thought they saw, turned out to be an alien spacecraft. It was on its way to its base in New Mexico. And then, – somebody, – decided to shoot that bogey down. – Ain't that right?"

"How'd you know that?" Asked a stunned young man.

"Let me continue. When the intellects discovered their mistake, they decided to cover their ass. It would stayed covered, except, those two deputies didn't go where I told them to go. Instead they made a joke of their investigation. When I saw those bodies and craft, I knew exactly who they were and how they got here. Now the governments got a little problem. The Venusians are a little unhappy about your mistake. Ain't that about right?"

"It's on the 'crypt-a-cone'," the old man affirmed. "And a whole lot more, if you know how to work it."
"I take it you know what a 'crypt-a-cone' is, and how to work it?" Asked Shawn.

"Yes, I know what a 'crypt-a-cone' is, and how it works, and I know in about two weeks those intellects are going to have a few saucers to deal with! Those Venusians are going to want their dead bodies and their space junk back! At least that's the gist I get from the 'crypt-a-cone', said the old man.

"We'll me to report this," said Shawn.

"You do that! I'm tired. You fellers go home." Then the old man added, "ain't talking no idiots, you get that?"

"Yes sir," said both young man.

CHAPTER THIRTY-FOUR

BELIEVE

A bout two days later, Shawn and Kevin returned. In the car was a man later identified as head of the space agency, – and David McFeen.

"Well look who's come calling!" The old man said vigorously shaking David's hand, and then came a gentleman hug. "My it's good to see you!"

"Mr. Boss," said the smiling David. "This is the director of scientific research of the space agency, – Mr. George Grissom, – I believe you've met Shawn and Kevin."

"You fellers come in and set a spell. I sure didn't expect David. How is your mother? – Your wife? – Little boss?" Asked the old man, smiling.

"Oh mom, she's fine. She says she's getting old. My wife is chasing after little boss, – and now Angie is on the way," David said, smiling.

"Angie?" Asked the old man. "I hadn't heard about Angie, – congratulations! What about Mattie? – Is she really married? Who would up with her?"

"Yeah, she married an Okie former. He's from our hometown and she's having a baby. – She's got a boy about three or so,

Lord help he's just like Mattie," said David. "And my little boss is now in school, – tearing up stuff."

After the warm reception it was time to get down to business.

"Mr. Boss," David said. "They asked me to come along, being as I know you. This is new territory for me and Mattie. Mattie was listening to the news the other day, when she heard that spoof about a reported flying saucer crash out in New Mexico. When your name and the location came to light, she made a couple of phone calls. It just had to be you. When Mattie talked to me, we thought maybe you was back in the gravitron business. But, this is something different, isn't it?"

"David, I got to ask, how much does your department know about us? About our work together?" Asked the old man.

"They know what little Mattie and I have told them, about our dad and his old boss. Mattie and I are doing research on 315. Why it don't stay stable under certain conditions, like full acceleration," said David.

"David," Mr. Grissom interrupted. "Does this man need to know all this? This is top-secret stuff."

"Sir," David said. "This man probably knows as much about 315 as anyone on earth. That's where Mattie and I got our education, in his barn."

"I stand corrected," said Mr. Grissom. "I didn't know."

"Mr. Boss," said David. "Can you tell me what this is all about? I'm in the dark."

"I'll try. I'll hit the high points. As you know, my wife and I moved out here about seven years ago, for her health. She died sometime back."

"I'm sorry," David said. "Mama told us about your loss."

"Anyway," continued the old man. "I got in the habit of walking all over this high desert around here, looking for artifacts and rocks to make arrowheads out of."

"We heard about that too," said David. "Mama has those shadow boxes on her wall that your wife sent."

"Well," continued the old man. "I was out on one of my safaris when I ran up on this dude taking soil samples as I supposed. We're not far from the Trinity site. He was a long way out from nowhere. I just didn't know what to make of him. He rattled in some kind of gibberish no human could understand. We set up some communication in points, grunts, and sign language. After a while, I started back home. Much to my surprise, he just kept in step. As we marched back to my home, it didn't take me long to figure out this dude ain't from around here. We kinda befriended each other, or, at least, an element of trust developed. I had heard about alien encounters out here in the desert, soon after we got here.

"Anyway, the third time I ran up on those strange dude's, I gave them a couple of boxes of my stone tools and arrowheads, I had made, and he gave me this 'crypt-a-cone'," said the old man, showing his audience his prize.

"A few days later, I took it over to the University for an appraisal as to what it was. They were just no help at all. They offered to send it somewhere. About six months later, I pitched a hissy fit and got it back. It came back with the insinuation that the 'crypt-a-cone' was a hoax from a space nut."

"That 'crypt-a-cone', – can you show me how it works?" David asked.

"Yes, but not until I tell you what to expect," said the old man. "Those strange marks are operating instructions in a Venusians dialect. I'll translate. Hold the device in both your hands, pointing the circle end toward your face. Count to three. Think of the question you want answered. The answer will appear in your head. When you're through asking questions, quit looking at the circle. A word of caution, don't ask too complicated a question. The answer may be overwhelming. There are a lot of earthly answers in that box. There's a lot more concerning Venus."

"David," the old man said. "You want to give this thing a try?"

"I'm almost afraid to. I don't like things messing around in my head. But, I trust you, and your say-so," David said. "I'll give it a try."

David took the device and looked at the circles, for maybe a minute or two. David exclaimed, "That's incredible! That's the most incredible thing I've ever seen! I just can't believe that. Can I do that again?" David asked.

"Be my guest. But be careful what you ask. You may get answers you don't want."

David took the device in his hands and began to stare at the circles, for another minute or so. When the session is over, David exclaimed as he handed the 'crypt-a-cone' back to Mr. Boss, "I just don't believe this! – That's incredible! – I just can't believe what I've just seen. – Mama is at home watching a soap opera on TV. – Mattie is working on gravitron. – My wife is with our children at the mall! All in real time. – Right now. I just don't believe it!"

"Mr. Grissom," the old man said. "You want to give this thing a try?"

"Is it safe?" Mr. Grissom asked, somewhat skeptical.

"It is unless you ask dangerous questions," said the old man smiling.

When Mr. Grissom, Shawn, and Kevin had their turns Mr.

Boss retrieved the device, did something, and put the device back in his pocket. All four men now were looking intently at the old man. – Maybe, – an explanation?

"Men," said the old man. "There are certain limits programmed into that box. It will not answer questions concerning Venusian technology. You'll get no response from the 'crypt-a-cone'. But nevertheless, there is a wealth of information in that box. It won't answer questions about 315. – You're on your own."

"All those bodies probably had a 'crypt-a-cone' on them, but they won't work. They've been deactivated as far as I know. This is the only 'crypt-a-cone' in captivity that works. As best as I can understand, this device is programmed to my brain. It works only on my authority. I saw the same images you saw. Kinda neat, don't you think? And, oh yeah, Kevin, Angela may say yes. Ah, Shawn you me to comment on, – you know?"

"Don't you dare!" Shawn said smiling.

"Mr. Grissom, I expected something more profound from you. Your retirement account?" Said the old man smiling.

"You've made your point," said Mr. Grissom annoyed "where does this take us?"

"Back to the Stone Age, if you shoot down another spaceship, or don't fulfill your contracts." Said the old man matter-of-factly.

"What contracts?" Demanded Mr. Grissom. "What contracts?"

"Those contracts the CIA made with the Venusians. I just know there are contracts. I didn't ask for the terms," the old man said.

"These Venusians," Mr. Grissom demanded. "How do you know they came from Venus?"

"When an alien points at Venus in the evening sky, you can kinda get the picture."

"Is that 'crypt-a-cone' the source of your information?" Mr. Grissom demanded.

"You want to use my 'crypt-a-cone' again and ask more questions?" The old man snarled. "Didn't you learn anything? That 'crypt-a-cone' is not the only source of information. Just look about! It's everywhere, you've been getting facts 1947. That Roswell thing should have been an eye-opener. Not a mind closer! Every time a UFO appears, the government dismisses it to the public as a flock of geese, a weather balloon, a hoax, or some other – aberration. – You could be learning something! Those aliens are not out to get you. Not once, not even once, has an alien encounter proven to be detrimental to human beings! The space hysteria we hear about comes from some damned government agency or maybe a horror movie!"

"You're mad," Mr. Grissom exclaimed. This whole thing is mad! I don't believe any of this!"

"Think so?" The old man pointed out. "Tell you what, let me borrow your 'crypt-a-cone' so I can get some answers."
"What are you getting at?" Mr. Grissom demanded. "What is the bottom line?"

"Oh you're a bottom line man," said the old man. "Well, here it is. Those Venusians aim to get their bodies and their space junk back. You can put up a fight, but I tell you, they have the means and the resolve to get them back. – And stay within the terms of those contracts! Earth is the closest planet to Venus. – They are here. – We are not there, and we have no means of getting there without stabilizing element 315."

"You've been in a fix since 1945. When mankind developed the means to destroy themselves with nuclear energy, – the universe took notice, – especially Venus. That cloud up there is the result of their nuclear winter. That planet was a habitable place until some damned mad Venusian pulled the trigger. They've been underground on Venus ever since. Since 1945, with the A-bomb, we've been on the same path they followed. Their technology is about 6000 years ahead of ours. They can explain a lot of things to you eggheads. If you can put two and two together, go read an ancient history book. Read the Bible, read Homer, mankind discovered the wheel, the pyramids were built. Look at the Mayan and Inca civilizations. In the West, all the indigenous people's legends in the Americas were full of alien encounters."

Then the old man added, "We're not alone out here on this mud ball. We're babes in the woods. Those aliens are not all out to get us. They might be of some help if we'll let them. But shooting down a spacecraft ain't no help, – either by design or accident! I don't know which it was, do you?"

"I can't answer that, I just don't know," said Mr. Grissom shaking his head. "I just don't know."

While Mr. Grissom and the old man were having this heated discussion David, Shawn, and Kevin were taking it all in. But they did not dare interrupt. This was a war between old dogs. It was just no place for puppies!

After a breathing spell Mr. Grissom asked, "How did you come to so much knowledge of element 315? That was developed in our laboratory, in Houston. David and Mattie were instrumental in its development."

"Mattie and David would of been my choice," said the old man smiling.

Mr. Grissom continued, "I've not been head of the developmental agency very long. I wasn't aware that anyone with your knowledge of 315 was outside of our agency. Initial research on element 315 and antigravity was done by David's father, one James McFeen and his confidant, his boss."

At last David piped up, "Mr. Grissom, that man is my daddy's confidant. That was my father's boss and friend, as he is mine and Mattie's. He's the man that advanced my father's work."

"I wasn't aware we were in the presence of greatness." Mr. Grissom said sarcastically.

"You're not! James McFeen was just a man that worked very hard as I used to. And, I might add, as David and Mattie do. No McFeen I've ever known has ever been blinded by self-importance. The McFeen's I know, just gets the job done!"

"I meant no offense," said Mr. Grissom. "It's just – it's just so mind-boggling. This alien thing, it's hard to accept. Such concepts! Surely you understand?"

"Maybe I do," said the old man. "Maybe I do, – I was a slow study too."

"Sir," Mr. Grissom asked. "How did you learn to deal with these aliens?"

"At first I thought it was just an accident," said the old man. "It didn't take me long to understand otherwise. When James left this earth in a make-shift spaceship, it got their attention. According to the 'crypt-a-cone', the Venusians have the means to monitor coming and goings in our solar system, like we do. When earth man, James, hit on antigravity, that made space flight possible. The fact that 315 is unstable, under certain conditions, is beside the point. Travel to other worlds was now a possibility, – just a matter of a short time.

"The Venusians took a real interest in James, when his homemade saucer creation began to travel around our solar system. Somehow they identified the people around him. Eventually they knew me and my association with James's work.

"Those Venusians had monitored that second saucer launch. It wasn't 10 feet off the ground before they knew about it. Irresponsible space travel is a threat to other worlds. My walks across the desert was my habit. My encounter with aliens was no accident. I did not know for certain until I was given the 'crypt-a-cone'. That 'crypt-a-cone', is a monitoring device also. Those aliens that crashed in 1947 had 'crypt-a-cones'. So did the ones the other day. Those Venusians have known your every move since 1947 with Roswell. Other intelligent aliens have been around for centuries. All you have to do is read the tea leaves."

After digesting this latest barrage of information, David asked, "Mr. Boss, those Venusians, what are they doing here?"

"Methane, it's vital to the Venusians existence. Humans have to have water. Venusians have to have methane. Earth has one of the greatest sources of methane in our solar system. Here's the key. Earth methane is underground. In the rest of the solar system, methane is in the atmosphere. Exactly how Venusians physiology works is unknown to me. I just take their word for it. The attraction is methane." The old man said. "Those Venusians have been mining methane on earth for centuries."

An exasperated Mr. Grissom exclaimed. "I don't believe this! This is preposterous. There is no science for methane in metabolism! This is contrary to everything known to science!"

"Fella," snarled the old man. "This is not something you've got to understand, but by God you're going to have to deal with these Venusians. You shot down one of their spacecraft. – Or at least, somebody did! The gist I get from the 'crypt-a-cone' is that was a breach of contract! I'm giving you an interpretation. I don't have any of the details. Things get lost in translation, from Venusian dialects to human language; their thought processes are different from human thought processes.

They're as much in the dark as we are about many aspects of our civilizations and our co-existence. The first seed sown to self-destruction is failure to consider another point of view, or the inherent danger of irresponsible actions."

At last Mr. Grissom observed, "I'm beginning to wonder if we know anything about anything. Venusians, methane, space-ships, all at one time! This is just too much! No wonder people have trouble believing these reports. I don't believe, – I just don't believe any of this. – Yet, – I'm afraid not to. Those bodies, that crashed spaceship, and that 'crypt-a-cone' demands a whole new realm of understanding. I came here looking for answers. All I have now is more questions, – I have no answers."

After Mr. Grissom had regained his composure the reality of an alien encounter, became apparent. "Sir," said Mr. Grissom. "This space crash reaches to the highest levels of our government. Our agency is for research and development, we don't make policy. Our agency don't shoot down flying saucers. We're just trying to build one. According to David and Mattie, you and James, have already built one and sent them into outer space. I don't know how much of this to believe. How could anyone believed that story? Yet, the demonstrations I have seen in Houston suggest this is the truth, – as hard as this is to believe."

"These Venusians," asked Mr. Grissom. "You say took a real interest in human development of nuclear energy in 1945, and with the subsequent development of spaceships. Are these things a threat to them?"

"According to my understanding, from the 'crypt-a-cone'," said the old man. "The advances in the new technology, nuclear energy, or in antigravity devices are secondary problems. It is the lack of responsible control of the new technologies that concerns them. Look at Chernobyl, Three Mile Island, or Fukushima, – it put Venus civilization underground. – That's nuclear run amok! Irresponsible space travel poses a similar threat, –

not only to ourselves, – but other worlds as well."

With antigravity technology, and with element 315 stable, the 67 million miles from Earth to Venus can be traveled in two weeks. Here to the moon would take thirty minutes. By every other conceivable means known to mankind at present, a trip to Venus would take nine months, – one way, – and the payload would be minuscule. But with 315 stable, the rules change in a heartbeat."

"That ship that was shot down, was a transport after a load of methane. Methane is vital to their existence. Now why, or how methane is of such importance, I don't know, but I don't know it is."

"The survivors of the Venus wars had to move underground. Their civilization on Venus is still underground, and their colonies on earth are underground."

"That nuclear explosion at Trinity site in 1945, sent shock waves through their processing concerns nearby. The Venusians have been monitoring the damage and residual radiation ever since. Somehow, since the Roswell thing in 1947, the Venusians reached an understanding with humans, but shooting down that transport upset the apple cart. In about two weeks, an armed armada will be here to protect their interest, that's what all this is about!"

According to the 'crypt-a-cone', there are two sites in the desert of New Mexico. That's why there are more sightings of UFOs in the great Southwest. There's very few people out West in comparison to back East. That's why nuclear energy came to life at Trinity in 1945. Distance is a safeguard and it provides security. The entrance to one of those colonies sites is near here. That's where that ship headed when it got shot down."

At last Mr. Grissom said, "I've got to report this, but I don't know who to report it to. And who is going to believe me?"

"Welcome to my world," the old man said.

"Mr. Boss," finally David asked. "Would you consider coming to Houston to help me and Mattie with 315?"

"Probably not," the old man said. "You and Mattie know as much as I do about 315. Besides, I'm just too damned old. The Venusians know about me and my whereabouts. They may decide to contact me. They have on three occasions."

At length it was time for the old man's visitors to leave. "Sir," said Mr. Grissom. "Shawn and Kevin will be your contact with any new information you might be privy to. You've been a tremendous service to our nation, and our space agency."

CHAPTER THIRTY-FIVE
NO EXPLANATIONS

T hings had quieted down for the old man. His blood pressure was beginning to calm down somewhat. A couple of months of peace and quiet, well-earned peace and quiet, were soon to be replaced with re-occurring chaos. When the old man's phone rang it was Mattie.

"Misser Boss," cooed Mattie. "It's so good to hear your voice. It's been so long, – way too long. So much has happened since last we talked. David filled me in on events out your way. I hope to see you soon, but right now, I'm a blimp. Our baby is due anytime. I have a three-year-old as well."

"David and I managed to get a few words in about old times and old friends, but as you know, the situation demanded other pressing considerations," the old man said.

After a few cordial minutes, Mattie stated the purpose of her call. "There have been some major developments in our agency. Mr. Grissom has been abruptly relieved as head of research. Shawn and Kevin have been reassigned and our research has been halted. David and I are out of a job with no explanation."

"After the baby gets here, my family and I, and David and his family, had talked about a long vacation. Maybe out in your area. At least until things settle down."

"Well you and David are all sure welcome in my world, since my wife died, I don't get many visitors. It would be nice to see old friends," said the old man.

"Misser Boss," Mattie said. "There's a lot more I need to say. David, Shawn, and Kevin will be out your way soon. – Thought I'd give you warning."

The next morning David, Shawn and Kevin arrived at the old man's house. "Mr. Boss," David said. "There is been a number of developments in the last couple of months. I'll hit the high points. There has been a rash of UFO sightings around the world of late. Those bodies and space junk just disappeared! The official line is that it never happened. Mr. Grissom was dismissed, and disgraced, as an idiot with a bad case of dementia. I guess you heard the news."

"Some," the old man said. "Enough to read between the lines, a big white wash is underway. The Russians probably did it, or maybe the Chinamen."

"I see you get the picture," said David. "What we're here about, – unofficially, – you understand, is a reference in one of those reports that there are two locations in New Mexico of alien activity. Do you by any chance know the location of that activity?"

"I can't show you the exact location of both front doors," the old man said smiling. "The one by Dulce has been rumored for years. There has been hundreds of reports over the years from up there, but no proof, as you know. The other may be within a mile of that crash site."

"Men," said the old man. "There was something about that crash site that don't add up. There is no answer on my 'crypt-a-cone'. What I find surprising was those bodies and wreckage was still there three days later. If their site is where I think their front door is, why didn't they pick-up those bodies and clean the area? That's what they usually do. – Unless that was staged, – for somebody's benefit. – Which leads to why?"

Shawn asked, "You think that was staged?"

"Could very well be, everything about this smells," the old man said, smiling. "Methinks me smells a rat. Them Venusians decided to make an issue out of human space travel. – Maybe it's not a good idea!"

After a short discussion, Kevin asked, "Could you show us the location of that front door? We brought some equipment. We came prepared to stay on that location for several days. – You know, – deer hunting."

"Well, lots of luck, there ain't no deer, but you might get cougar ate. I've seen tracks. David, you deer hunting too?" Asked the old man.

"Not this time. I'm an errand boy. When I get back to Houston, I got to report to Mattie. She's a little impatient of late, – no, a whole lot impatient!" David said, smiling. "My flight leaves in about three hours. Maybe I'll be back in a few days. Maybe Mattie will be up and about by then. It's going to be a girl. I just don't think the world is ready for another Mattie."

"Seems I remember she was always a little impatient at times, maybe a baby will slow her down for a while," said the old man smiling.

<><><><><><>

Shawn and Kevin retrieved their very large backpacks from the car and their large suitcases. "My word," said the old man. "You going to tote all that stuff?"

"We may be there a while," said Kevin.

"What do you want to do for water?" The old man asked.

"We have a re-claimer here. It extracts moisture from the air. They were real good back East in high humidity. Out here, who knows?" Said Shawn.

"Well don't plan on no baths, – and plan on staying downwind from me," the old man said smiling.

The old man gathered up his hoe and water. "I ain't staying out there in those snakes after dark. You can have my share. I got all I want right here. I get `um up on my front porch, I get `um on my back porch, I get `um in my garage, – they're just everywhere! They come slithering out after dark. I don't get out much after dark."

"What kind of snakes?" Kevin asked, wide-eyed.

"Rattlesnakes, for starters, about six different varieties. And then there are bull snakes, King snakes, Adler's, Hogg noses and, just snake snakes, – and uh, – creepy snakes," said the old man smiling.

"That's just not very reassuring," said Kevin.

"Oh, did I mention beaded lizards and Gila monsters? They are about too," said the old man still smiling. "Oh well, – do you remember where that crash site was?"

"I think so," Shawn said. "I'll remember that site as long as I live."

"We'll see," said the old man. "You're not the only visitor out there these days. The Venusians took a look see out there a few days ago."
"Have you been back out there?" Asked Kevin.

"Don't need to, I saw the ships come and go a few days ago," said the old man. "My guess is that site was picked cleaner than I hounds tooth. I'll bet your every move was monitored and recorded on a 'crypt-a-cone'."

"We're hoping so. We're hoping they know that. That's why we're here." Said Shawn. "Maybe they'll contact us, like they did you, there has been other contacts in the past."

"Sir," said Shawn. "Not everyone in the space agency enjoyed or ignored your report. Some folks in other departments took them very serious indeed. Our lab knew in a second what that 'crypt-a-cone' was. They had seen them before."

"Uh Hu, and just what else did somebody know about space aliens?" The old man asked.

"A lot," said Shawn. "Aliens have been on top of our departments list since the Roswell thing in 1947."

As the men continued their hike across the rough terrain, the old man noticed the young bucks were laboring under their heavy backpacks, and suitcases. "Ain't you fellers tuckered out yet? I need to set a spell. – You know old age," the old man said smiling.

The old man sat down on a rock, Kevin and Shawn sat down on their suitcases.

"I'm beginning to get a clearer picture of what's been happening. I'm kind of a slow steady," said the old man. "There's been a fly in the ointment, from the get-go. Now you're the fly trap and I've been the bait, ain't that about it?"

"That's about it unfortunately for you," said Shawn. "When James McLean developed that saucer back in the 80s, and it left Earth, the Venusians were not the only ones who took note. – We're still tracking that saucer, – that was a very thorough investigation. Anything leaving our solar system got somebody's undivided attention. Those books and that dictionary, were poured over by countless people, but when you unraveled that mystery we were still in the dark. That saucer of yours wasn't ten feet off the ground before somebody knew it. And those two kids, what can I say?"

"Uh Hu," mused the old man, after considering this latest bit of information. "315, that's it! You got the kinks worked out. – That's what this is all about. Ain't it? That bunch in Houston, where David and Mattie worked, – they got the kinks out of 315! – And now, – the Venusians are a little excited about it. – They are afraid earthlings will be irresponsible!"

"That's about the size of it," said Shawn.

After some deep consideration, the old man asked, "What you need me for? What's my part in all this? "

"You supply the missing pieces. We knew they were here. We knew about where they were. But, we didn't know what they were after methane, – that of all things, – that was the missing link. We don't know what they need it for, but we now know they do. There are large deposits of methane around Dulce, there once was near here. We're hoping to find the site near here. We think it's a processing plant, or maybe they are just observing the Trinity site residual radiation. Maybe our efforts will shed some light on what they are doing," said Shawn.

"Lots of luck." After some thought, while continuing their hike, the old man asked. "By chance do you know where those saucers are now?"

"We know," confirmed Shawn. "They are not around here."

<><><><><>

When the men reached the crash site, there was nothing to see. Everything was as it once was. The mesquites, chollas, and prickly pears showed no sign of any disturbance, – whatsoever. All traces of human activity was gone. Where the helicopters had landed, no evidence was discernible.

"I see what you mean," said Kevin. "It's clean as hound's

tooth."

"It takes a while, if you're really observant," said the old man. "But, you can see where they've been. The entrance to their front door is about a mile from here. Those folks are masters of camouflage, as you can see."

"How did you come across the entrance of their location?" Kevin asked.

"I used think by luck. I'm just not so sure now. It was my second encounter with aliens. I was out in the desert looking for rocks, when I ran up on some odd footprints, – two sets. They led the way I wanted to go, but they disappeared at a rock. People can't walk through a rock. Those rocks looked like something walked through the rock. When later, I returned to the location, on my way home, those unusual tracks were gone. When the wind blows or it rains, everything disappears in the desert, but there was no wind or rain that day. We're headed for that rock, we'll be there soon."

The men made their way up the ravine. At last the old man announced, "Well, here it is. I have poked around your some. I don't think that rock is a rock. It don't sound right when you whoop it. I'll show you what I mean."

The old man picked up a nearby rock, and bounced it off the rock, but no sound emitted. "You catch the difference?" The old man asked.

"There was no sound, – and look, – there's not even a scratch where you hit it," said Kevin all eyes.

"I take it you've got some way to unravel this mystery?" The old man asked.

"We're going to try," Shawn said. "We're going to camp out here to start the deer hunt."

"Want me to check up on you men in a few days?" The old

man asked.

"It won't be necessary. Our whereabouts will be monitored," said Shawn. – "At least we hope so!"

"Somebody will be watching," the old man mused. "I guess I'll mosey on home."

213

CHAPTER THIRTY-SIX
NO MORE

A couple of months passed by, it was now late fall. The desert monsoon was ended and the coolness of winter was well on its way. The old man was gazing out his window, looking for any sign of activity. Even in the night skies nothing was unusual. An occasional shooting star would be seen. No meteor sightings have been reported since last summer. There was a couple of vague and unsubstantiated UFO sighting, from the Dulce area in the local news.

The old man had been out on his desert walks occasionally. The weather was cooling down and the snakes were back in their dens. A few days after he had left Shawn and Kevin at their deer hunt location, he returned. As he cleared the rise where the rock was, no traces of human existence were evident. Shawn and Kevin, and all their stuff was simply gone.

<><><><><>

It was nearing Thanksgiving when the big SUV came through the gate. The young man and the young woman, carrying a baby, got out all smiles.

"Mattie is that you? Is it really you?" The old man said excited.

"Misser Boss, this is my husband Jimmy McCullen. – You

may not remember him, but his dad was a Mis Fit," said Mattie.

"My, my, you were a knee nibbler the last time I saw you. How's Walter?" Asked the old man.

"He passed away three years ago," said Jimmy.

"And who might this be?" The old man asked, as Mattie passed the baby to the old man's waiting arms.

"That's Margaret. We named her after my mother," said Mattie smiling. – We thought we'd drop by, – we're on vacation. We'll be going home next week. Back to Oklahoma, – the old home place, – were farmers now, cows, horses and kids."

"No more gravitron?" The old man asked.

"From all accounts," Mattie said. "Officially, from all accounts, gravitron and 315 never existed. It's just something no one ever heard of. – Not in Houston, – not in Oklahoma, – not anywhere. After our research agency was abruptly shut down, David finally got a job back in Tulsa, in computers. I just quit looking. It's like Houston never existed. Any reference to gravitron is now met with skepticism, ridicule, or as space nuts. It's just like in the old days, when daddy disappeared. Nobody believes a word you say, so we just quit talking about it."

"We all know that trick," the old man said. "I've said all I aim to say about it too."

ABOUT THE AUTHOR

D.w. Smith

Doyle Smith began writing by keeping a notebook handy as a young man. Over the many years a considerable stack of 'stuff' accumulated.

His first published work at seventy-four, – was a short story collection, Tales From Rattlesnake Gulch, 2017. Followed by My, My, 2018, another short story collection. His first novel, Gold, Ghosts, And Woollys, was published in 2019.

James, a science-fiction novel, is due for publication, in 2020 as is Homer, another novel.

Doyle, now older than dirt, stays active doing church and community service, and taking long walks in the desert near San Antonio, New Mexico. – Yes! There is a San Antonio, New Mexico. – It's near Rattlesnake Gulch, where Doyle, a transplanted Okie, now lives and writes.

BOOKS BY THIS AUTHOR

Tales From Rattlesnake Gulch

A Collection of humorous Short Stories

My, My

More Short Stories

Gold, Ghosts, And Woolly's

A Grandfather's Tale to his grandson. A story all ages will enjoy.

Made in the USA
Columbia, SC
11 August 2024

39876976R00131